LILA AND THERON

LILA AND THERON

Bill Schubart

Charles Michael Publishing

Inspired by a story by Claire Hancock
Front Cover Photograph by Richard Brown
Literary Editor: Lin Stone
Copyeditor: Brian Bendlin

Manufactured in the United States of America
Book design and typeformatting by Bernard Schleifer

ISBN13: 9781682613566
ISBN10: 1682613569

AUTHOR'S NOTE

This is the backstory to "Lila's Bucket," which appears in *The Lamoille Stories*, and "Lila's Death" and "Lila's Burial," which appear in *The Lamoille Stories II*.

This is a work of fiction, but like most works of fiction, it is based on some real events and real people.

For Claire

THE DISAPPEARING WORLD

*Lila and Theron do not imagine themselves
poor, nor do they covet what they don't have.
They are whole in themselves and on their land
and progress impinges little on their lives.*

Be cold
Forage and grow
Haul wood and stone
Go hungry
Use hand tools
Be bold
Raise children
Cure food
Walk without light
Keep animals
Grow old
Adore someone
Greet wildlife
Pay rapt attention
Forgive yourself and others

Blessed are the meek, for they shall inherit the earth.
　　　　　　　　—MATTHEW 5:5, the Third Beatitude

ACKNOWLEDGMENTS

HEARTFELT THANKS ARE DUE TO MY CRITICAL READERS: Will Patten, Denise Shekerjian, Tom Slayton, Anna Stevens, and Lin Stone; this book would not be what it is without your perceptive and thoughtful feedback and criticism. Lin Stone went above and beyond as a mentor and literary editor, offering vital feedback, support, and encouragement as the manuscript took shape. My gratitude also goes to Arvo Pärt, one of our greatest contemporary composers, whose *Berliner Messe* and *Spiegel im Spiegel* enriched the narrative timbre as I wrote the book. My gratitude to logger, storyteller, and author Bill Torrey for reviewing passages about logging and log runs.

Special thanks is reserved for my sister, Claire Hancock, the keeper of so many family stories, including much of this one, and finally to her grandchildren, Lila and Theron, my grand niece and nephew, who kindly lent their beautiful names to this work of fiction.

LILA AND THERON

PROLOGUE

*H*ARDWOOD *F*LATS *DOESN'T APPEAR ON MOST LOCAL MAPS,
but the name is used by locals to describe an unmapped
area between Elmore, Wolcott, and Woodbury. It's a hard-
scrabble mix of isolated ponds, marshland, mixed second-growth
hardwoods, and occasional stands of young evergreens.
Walking in the woods, one can always hear running water
somewhere. Much of the terrain seems to float on an inland
sea. Here and there, a few dirt roads, passable except in mud
season, wind through the woods, feeding into corduroy
logging roads and then tapering off into hunting trails and
deeryards. Occasional year-round dwellings nestle here and
there on the passable roads. Hunters or hikers will sometimes
run across abandoned farmhouses moldering in clearings
marked by their overgrown lilac bushes or unpruned apple
trees. Farther in, they may encounter a tarpaper deer camp
with sun-bleached antler racks over a padlocked door.

1

THELMA DIES AT NINETEEN GIVING BIRTH TO A SON,
Theron. When the son first meets his father, he
learns his mother's death is his fault and can only
muster the question, "How did she die?"

Looking away, the father mutters, "She died givin'
birth ta you. An' I lost all her help and comforts."

Lionel Wright and Thelma Norris have been shy
sweethearts since sixth grade in the one-room Elmore
Standard School and, in high school, their schoolmates
see them as a couple. Lionel proposes to Thelma just
as the shadow of financial depression overspreads the
land. They know they can better manage adversities
together. Three months later, Thelma is pregnant. The
Elmore church ladies retail the couple's mortal sin to
a few deaf ears in town, but in parlous times, it's not
uncommon for children to come hard on the heels of
marriage, as few childless farms or marriages survive.

The following year, Lionel and Thelma buy a
thirty-four-acre property with an empty farmhouse, an
eighteen-stanchion barn with a small hayloft and half
a dozen barn cats, and a henhouse on stilts from the
local bank shortly after their wedding. Only twelve

acres are cleared for haying or pasture; Lionel hopes to clear another six that remain dry most of the year. Thelma's father gives them nine freshened Jerseys and Guernseys from his dwindling herd, and neighbors in Hardwood Flats give them a motley collection of laying hens. Lionel's uncle Clemson brings a pregnant sow and a swaybacked Belgian draft horse named Luther, trained for logging, as wedding gifts. Within days of their union in the town clerk's office, followed by a small gathering on the lawn outside, Lionel and his new bride have a starter farm.

Thelma knows how to garden, churn butter, preserve, and cellar root vegetables. Every year since she was eleven, she's won prizes at the fair for her blackberry preserves and apple and maple butters. Uncle Clemson taught Lionel how to barrel and age sap beer without blowing up a root cellar, even though Lionel avoids spirits.

Twice a week Lionel drives his buckboard to a neighbor's farm, where he leaves four milk cans to be collected by the creamery route truck from Morristown. On the off days, the cans stand chilling in the same oaken spring box above the house that feeds water to the cast-iron sink in the kitchen.

In early fall, Lionel returns one Tuesday to find Thelma passed out on the kitchen floor in a puddle of her own blood. She doesn't respond to his cries to her as he lifts her head in his arms. He unhooks Luther from his traces, mounts him, and gallops the five miles into Morristown. Forty minutes later, Doc Jewett's black buggy pulls up and he rushes into the house.

"She's gone," he says softly to Lionel. "I'm sorry. You couldn't a' done any different. She was bleedin' internally, and 'less I had 'er at the Copley, I couldn't a' done anything to save her. I'm so sorry."

Doc Jewett raises Thelma's cotton dress to her torso and, not surprised to find no undergarments, uses forceps from his black leather bag to extract a silent male infant. He cuts and ties off the blue umbilical cord attaching the child to his dead mother, and with a black rubber bulb removes the bloody mucus from the child's nose and throat. Holding him by his ankles, he slaps him several times on the back until the surprised infant lets out a howl. The doc wipes the full-throated newborn clean with an unbloodied section of Thelma's dress and swaddles him in a quilt from the couch. He then hands Lionel his newborn son and tells him to keep him warm until he can return with his nurse, Elise Jackson, and Jack Shank, the undertaker.

His wife of less than a year now gone, Lionel's earlier doubts about happiness come back. "Too good to last," he tells himself.

"How do I feed 'im?" Lionel asks Doc Jewett.

"'Lise'll bring some breast milk to get him quieted down."

"Then what?" pouts Lionel, stifling the sobs deep in his chest.

"Step at a time, Lionel. Wanda Demars just had a baby girl. Maybe she can nurse two for a while 'til your son can tolerate some a' that nice, rich Jersey milk you got out there in the barn," answers Doc.

"He don' feel like my son what with 'is mother gone," mumbles Lionel. "She died givin' birth to 'im. What's 'at say 'bout 'im?"

"Don't talk that way, Lionel. Mothers die in childbirth. It's not the child's fault. This'll come 'round and I'll be 'round to help. Be patient. Y'ave a son."

Alone, after hearing Doc Jewett's buggy clatter off, Lionel takes the first of many drinks from a green-tinted bottle his snickering school friends brought him at his wedding. They'd camouflaged the bottle, filled with clear corn liquor, in a shoebox so no one would suspect its illicit contents. Their smirks at the makeshift reception alerted Lionel to its contents, and he took it home, still wrapped. He'd often hinted at his disdain for liquor, even as friends were trying it out for the first time. Elmore, Wolcott, and Morrisville are "dry towns," by annual voice vote at the town meeting, though even "dry votes" are known to betray a thirst for spirits.

Elise Jackson accompanies Jack Shank in his horse-drawn hearse. She rushes into the house and takes charge of the newborn that Lionel has settled on the couch alone, still wrapped in the quilt. Through the window she spots Lionel in the backyard, staring south toward Elmore Mountain. She calls to him, but gets no response. With his son in her arms, she walks down the back steps and approaches Lionel, who doesn't acknowledge her presence. She's surprised to smell liquor and, when he finally turns to confront her, she sees a glazed, faraway look. She knows it's best to leave him be, and returns to the kitchen, where Jack has already laid Thelma out in the simple coffin he's brought. He's mopping up the substantial pool of blood on the linoleum floor and wringing the reddened rag mop into the iron sink by hand, his bare forearms pink with Thelma's blood.

Elise sets the bottle of mother's milk she brought from the hospital into the kettle bubbling over the still-warm fire. The newborn boy cradled in her right arm is quiet now but breathing steadily. She thinks to herself, "It's better Lionel be outside," but she's disturbed by the smell of alcohol on him.

Jack goes out to talk with Lionel. Lionel hasn't moved. Jack sees the green-tinted bottle sitting in the grass at his feet.

"I'm sorry, Lionel," Jack offers. "She was much too young to die like that. It don' seem fair."

" 'S my fault for not bein' 'ere with 'er, her time so close and all. I shoulda been 'ere, but had ta take the milk cans down ta Lester's for pickup. My fault, don'cha know. What 'm I gonna do wi' that young 'un in there? Never raised no kid, can't nurse 'im. Ya might's well take 'im with 'is mother. How's 'e gonna live, knowin' 'e caused 'is mother ta die? Tell me that."

"Lionel, it'll come right in time. I've seen this before. Elise'll take the young boy with her and see he gets off to a good start. You take care a' things here, make a home for him and choose a name for your son. I'm gonna go now. I'll take Thelma to the funeral home. I know ya haven't got any money, bein' a newlywed with a new mortgage 'n' all. I'll talk to the overseer and we'll make a nice sendoff for Thelma. Don'cha worry on it. Which preacher ya want there? I know you ain't religious, but in a small town ya gotta have someone to say the last words."

"I can pay ya, but it'll take some time. Pick any preacher, maybe that holy codger at the Congo church. We wasn't church folks much, tho' Ma was raised Cath'lic 'fore she crossed the border and married Dad. God, seems like a hunnerd years ago now, and here I is, alone and married with a young'un."

Lionel drops to his knees and begins sobbing. Jack places a hand on Lionel's shoulder, at a loss as to what to say. He pats him once, then returns to the house. Elise is trying to introduce a rubber nipple to Lionel's newborn son with no success. She shakes loose a drop of milk onto the tip and sets the hard nipple on the baby's lips.

Meanwhile, Jack jockeys a coffin hand truck under one end of the maple coffin. The homemade contraption enables him to wheelbarrow a coffin to the hearse. It's harder with a corpse inside, especially negotiating the narrow stairways in old farmhouses. On more than one occasion he's spilled his cargo, to the horror of the dead person's kin, but he usually has help. Thelma had been a sturdy but slight woman, and he's able to load her alone into the hearse, while Elise settles into the adjacent seat with her charge back in full howl. Over the racket the two try to discuss the situation, finally deciding it best to leave Lionel to his grief for now and come back the following day with more answers—and more questions.

2

A T THELMA'S FUNERAL, LIONEL STANDS RAMROD straight in the back of the Congregational church. The front pews are vacant, as there's no family to attend except his brother Adrian and his uncle Clemson, who stand with him at the back of the church near the stairs to the organ loft. Folks in town who know Lionel's circumstances or were close to Thelma in school come to help fill the empty pews. There are more white-painted churches in town than people to fill them, as most were built at a more observant time in the town's history.

Lionel's son Theron, perhaps because of his difficult birth, grows into a vigorous infant. Wanda Demars provides bountiful nourishment for both her newborn daughter and for Theron in his first few months. Elise arranges for other mothers in Wanda's neighborhood to take the boy for brief periods, so Wanda can have time alone with her daughter and her husband Dwayne, who works as the county fence viewer and is often away.

Leonard Fogg is the town's elected overseer of the poor. He and Elise see to Lionel during his grieving. Although they worry about his being alone out in the Flats with so few neighbors, they know Lionel comes from resilient stock.

When Theron comes home to the Flats, he's "weaned, cleaned, and ready to grow," according to Elise. She's secured a used cradle, some hand-me-down baby clothes, a dozen cotton diapers, two glass baby bottles, and a little bag of safety pins. She spends the first hour explaining to Lionel the basics of infant care. Elise can tell, however, that Lionel's distracted; she looks up to affirm his understanding and sees him staring out the window toward the silvering woodpile seasoning in the sun or toward the barn, where his cows have begun lowing to be milked.

She leaves, promising to return the following day. The next day, however, widow Grenier falls and breaks her hip in her apartment on Portland Street. This consumes much of Elise's day, so she puts off her return until the following morning. With so few comings and goings in the Flats, she has no way of notifying Lionel that she's had to delay her home visit.

Elise arrives at eight o'clock the following morning and smells coffee brewing. Lionel answers her call at the door with a nod to come in. His son lies on his back in the cradle, howling, his pale chubby limbs flailing the fetid air. A yellowish goo leaks from the edge of his diaper and a bottle of milk lies nearby. Elise can see that the crib sheet is wet and dirty and the fire that Lionel has started in the woodstove barely radiates any heat into the chilly kitchen. Lionel looks away, ashamed. He's drawn breach calves from their moaning mothers, has bottle-fed orphaned piglets, but his own son is a stranger to him, seemingly there only to remind him of losing the one person he loved.

Elise understands Lionel can't manage his own grief and his new son's care. What she doesn't see yet is that Lionel connects the two and that it will be years before he forgives his son.

Lionel offers Elise a cup of coffee that she takes with a smile.

"Let's chat a minute 'fore you head off to work," she says. "I want your permission to take your son and make arrangements for his care 'til he reaches an age where he can manage on his own, rejoin you when he's older and won't make demands on your farm work. I know how hard you work to make a go of it and I know, too, you'll be a fine father to the boy. I also know that care at this age is a woman's work, and Thelma's no longer here to do it."

"Hard to forget that," mutters Lionel.

"I know, but time heals all. I lost my father when I was seven and it took me 'til I was married before I stopped missing him every day."

"I spoke with Leonard," Elise continues, "and he's agreed. He 'sured me he can find a good home in town for young Theron and get 'im a mother's care 'til he's old enough to come home to you and help on the farm."

"I gotta go clean out the gutters and fork down some hay. Thanks fer all yer help and understandin'. I can care for him when he's growed a bit, but I've always been scared of babies. Know that sounds funny, but they seem, I dunno . . . breakable or sumpin'. I coun't make him stop cryin' last night, and I got angry, scared myself, and went to bed. I know I done wrong, but din't know what to do ta make it right."

Lionel hangs his head and Elise sees the moisture in his eyes as he sets his enameled tin coffee cup on the edge of the stove and leaves for the barn. She adds some hot water from the tea kettle simmering on the stove to a basin of cool water in the iron sink. She removes Theron's dirty diaper, folds it up and sets it on the floor, then cleans him up with some warm soapy water. The warmth surprises him, and his howling stops. She puts on a new diaper and changes his little nightshirt. She then wraps him in a small quilt and carries him to her buggy. She lays him on its wood floor and returns to get the supplies she brought earlier.

A few minutes later, Lionel hears Elise driving off with his son down the two-track road leading out of the Flats. It's unusual for Lionel to hear more than one or two buggies a week pass his farm. He pauses in the hayloft and takes a nip from the pint of blackberry brandy in his coverall pocket.

3

THERON THRIVES IN THE CLEVELAND FAMILY. AT Elise's request, Leonard Fogg, as county overseer, has arranged for a modest support payment to Linwood and Emma Cleveland for adding Theron to their own brood of three. There's plenty of room in their rambling farmhouse, and an infant adds little to the child-rearing chores. Becky and Linda are eleven and thirteen, and each now has her own live doll to tend, as their youngest brother, Ben, has just turned two. Like many hill farms, the Clevelands' dairy is marginal, so Linwood augments his milk check working part-time on the town road crew, clearing culverts, disposing of roadkill, and clearing roadside rights-of-way. Leonard's eight-dollar monthly stipend for caring for Theron buys a week's worth of groceries for the whole clan.

Leonard and Elise visit twice a year to see how Theron's progressing and to assess when he should rejoin his father. Leonard also checks in with Lionel each spring to see how he's faring alone in the Flats.

When Theron turns six, Leonard and Elise decide it's time to reconsider his foster arrangement.

Theron will enter first grade the following fall, and should do so from the home in which he'll be raised. Their assessment of Lionel's circumstances is largely positive: he's added to his herd and is now milking eighteen; he has a good supply of hay and wood and, on the morning Leonard comes by, it's toasty in Lionel's kitchen even though it's thirty degrees outside.

When people need to reach Lionel, they enlist his neighbor Neal, who lives farther in on Flats Road, to drop off a note in Lionel's mailbox on his way home from town. Leonard sends word that he and Elise will be dropping by Thursday morning to discuss Theron's return. The note makes Lionel nervous. He's become used to living alone, though often, as he lies in bed at night, he finds himself wondering about the boy he hasn't seen for five years.

Elise and Leonard arrive in Elise's buggy. Lionel has a bluestone enamel pot of coffee boiling hard on the stove.

Leonard opens the discussion, saying he thinks it's time Lionel and his son are reunited. He notes that Lionel is doing well enough, and the Cleveland family's done a fine job rearing Theron so far, but that now it's time for him to join his kin, especially since he'll be starting school in September.

Lionel nods as he pours coffee into three cups and sets a pint mason jar of sugar and another of cream on the oak table. Elise notices Lionel pouring a dark liquid out of another mason jar by the sink into his own cup of coffee and suspects it's liquor. Facing Leonard, she nods toward Lionel. Leonard nods, indicating he saw the same. Leonard is forthright.

"You drinkin' much?" he asks Lionel.

"What's it to ya?" retorts Lionel. "None yer business, is it? I takes a nip now 'n' agin, special when it's cold."

"Warm enough in 'ere," answers Leonard. "No need to be drinkin' this early, is 'ere?"

"Mind yer own beeswax! Just tell me when Theron's comin' home. I'll need to make 'im a room ready 'n' all."

"Is 'ere anything you'll need that ya don' have to care for Theron? You got school clothes for him, as he'll be going to school this coming fall. You got enough food for two?"

"We'll make do wi' both. What day's 'e comin' home?"

"How about this Sunday?" asks Leonard.

"Fine by me. I ain' goin' nowhere. I'll be here when ya bring'm."

"We'll be goin' now. Sure everthin's all right, Lionel?" asks Leonard.

"Why woun't it be?" growls Lionel, putting his cup down hard on the edge of the stove.

"See ya don' let the drink make away with ya,

like it does ta some," says Leonard. "Theron needs a dad. We'll be goin' now. C'mon, Elise."

Lionel doesn't acknowledge their departure but refills his coffee cup with coffee, adding an equal amount of brandy.

Leonard turns to Elise, whose buggy is bouncing through the deep ruts on Flats Road and says, "I don' like that Lionel's drinking this early in the morning; you best keep an eye out."

"I will," promises Elise.

4

THERON'S ANXIETY ABOUT LEAVING THE CLEVE-lands grows when Ben, his best friend and ally, begins school in Sterling and Theron finds himself alone during the day, occasionally helping out Emma when asked. In large families preoccupied with day-to-day subsistence, parents must limit their family time, and children figure out their roles early on. To many children, this independence is a blessing; but Theron, already orphaned once, feels more alone. Theron and Ben are close, and Theron yearns to go to school with his friend but is too young. As he watches his foster siblings file out the front door with their homework straps and lunch bags, he imagines himself joining them.

Theron's anxiety worsens when Linwood, Emma, and Leonard sit him down after supper the following week to tell him he'll be returning to his real home to live with his father. Theron has no memory of his father or his house. When he came to live with Linwood and Emma they felt—and Elise and Leonard agreed—that it would be easier on him and his foster family not to explain the circumstances of his adoption until he's older.

What Theron learns from his life in a foster family raises more questions for him about his own mother and father. When he begins asking questions, he's told his father couldn't care for him when he was born; he's told only that his mother died young and that his father was too busy and bereft to care for a young child after just starting out in farming and then losing his young wife. He's not told she died giving birth to him.

On hearing of the decision in which he'll have no say, Theron's first question is, "Will there be other kids?"

Emma Cleveland breaks the silence, promising him he'll meet many kids when school starts the following fall.

"Will I go to the same school as Ben?" Theron persists.

"Ben goes to school here in Sterling, and you'll be going in Elmore, where your dad lives. If you both work hard and go on to high school, you'll see each other there," Emma answers, smiling.

This is the first Theron hears of school as a measurement of elapsed time and he wonders how far in the future "high school" is, adding to his sense of uncertainty.

The following Sunday, Emma roasts a fresh ham with potatoes for family dinner and invites Leonard and Elise. The plan is that after dinner, they'll all say their good-byes and Leonard and Emma will drive Theron to meet his father.

Ben and Emma help him pack his suitcase the night before. In the steel-frame bed they've shared for five years, Theron and Ben talk long into the night. Ben knows Theron is crying and holds him, promising they'll visit each other. But both know that their plans will always be subject to the will of grown-ups who can rarely find the time to indulge them.

The Cleveland family all wave good-bye as Elise drives off down Sterling Brook Road. Theron sits beside her with his suitcase under his left arm. After forty-five minutes, Theron begins to worry about how long it takes to ride from the Cleveland Farm to his father's house, inferring that his new home is a long way from the one he's leaving. They pass a narrow lake and then enter a new-growth forest. He learns from Elise that this wood is called "the Flats" and this will be his new home. The ride stretches even longer as Elise negotiates the two-track road deeper into the woods.

The Cleveland Farm sits on the side of Sterling Mountain and is surrounded on three sides by open meadow with distant views of the Worcester Range. But in the Flats there's no view—only what's ahead and behind as they penetrate deeper into the woods. Theron's anxiety turns to fear, but he can see Elise glancing sideways at him and he's determined not to cry.

When Elise reins her horse into a pull-off, Theron sees a farmhouse in a clearing through some white birch whips, and he knows this is the place. Elise wraps the reins around a birch and hops off to help Theron down from the buggy seat. She takes Theron's suitcase and hand, assuring him, "Everythin'll be fine. Your pa's waitin' for ya."

Theron accompanies Elise up a slight rise and along a path through the birches. Theron surveys his new home. It's smaller than the Cleveland farmhouse, but well-kept, and it has retained most of its white paint. There's a porch in the front but no one in sight. Theron's hand grips Elise's again and she responds by repeating, "Everythin'll be fine."

They climb the steps, and Elise knocks on the edge of the screen door.

"C'min," Theron hears. "I'm right 'ere. C'mon in. No need to stand on the porch."

Elise pushes Theron ahead of him into the kitchen. Leonard is having coffee with Lionel. Elise sets down Theron's suitcase and says, "Lionel, meet your son, Theron. He's a fine boy, and he's been looking forward to comin' home."

Theron stares at the scuffed linoleum floor. Lionel walks toward his son, extending a calloused hand. Theron looks up at the hand and puts his inside it. Lionel shakes his hand, saying, "We gotta build up that grip a yourn, make a man a' ya."

Leonard smiles, and Elise cautions, "He's still a boy, Lionel. No need ta work him too hard just yet.

35

There's plenty a' time for that when he's grown a bit. He'll be strong like his dad, but all in good time. Next fall you want to concentrate on his learnin' and gettin' by in school and makin' new friends. He's bound to miss 'is first kin. He'll go to the Elmore Standard. Meanwhile, you two can spend the time gettin' to know one another as father and son. Why don'cha show your son his new room?"

Lionel lifts the burner lid, tosses a split of white ash into the stove, and resettles the lid. He takes the leather hide suitcase and climbs the narrow staircase. "Follow me," he says to his son.

Theron looks nervously at Leonard, who nods at the staircase and smiles. "It's fine, son, follow your dad. He'll show you your new room."

The two disappear up the narrow staircase, and Leonard suggests to Elise that they leave while the two are upstairs. Elise disagrees, saying she wants to be sure Theron's okay and to say good-bye to him and assure him that she'll be around if he needs help getting used to his new circumstances.

"Sometimes it's best just to go," Leonard says, but he nonetheless accedes to Elise's wish.

The two return a few minutes later without the suitcase. Theron looks no less anxious.

5

THERON AND LIONEL'S FIRST WINTER TOGETHER lasts deep into April.

The first snow falls late one night in the second week of November. There's a respite when it melts in a brief sunlit warm spell, but then snow returns with a vengeance. Sixteen inches fall before Thanksgiving Day, on which father and son share a roast partridge Lionel shoots while picking the last of the apples.

Theron's quiet most of the time, and Lionel's content with the silence, with which he's familiar. Theron hears what he needs to hear from his father, enough to know what and when to do the things his father needs done, such as refilling the firewood box next to the Glenwood stove, fetching root vegetables from the cellar and cleaning them in the sink for Lionel to cook, or helping him open bales and fork hay to "the girls" or fetching eggs from "the biddies." Sometimes Theron wonders if there's another person in their house, as he hears his father talking to someone. The one-sided conversations increase as the days shorten.

Theron's too young to do the milking, and Lionel looks forward to the day when his son can learn it and eventually do the task on his own. For now, though, the barn is the only place Lionel feels comfortable drinking.

Theron misses the variety of meals he was used to at the Clevelands. For dinner, Emma usually prepared three or four different things to put on the plates: meat, potatoes or beans, a vegetable, a saucer of her homemade sweet pickles, bread, and, at supper time, a pie, cake, or Sunday's donuts, still rich with the shortening she simmered them in.

Theron's meals with his father are typically boiled turnips, carrots, potatoes, or parsnips with butter, salt, and milk. Occasionally Lionel thaws a piece of cached venison or beef from the metal trash can just outside the kitchen door or he beheads, plucks, and cleans a spent hen from the coop. The icebox in the corner of the kitchen is used mostly for keeping grains and beans from mice, as harvesting ice in winter is too much work and there are no ice deliveries in the Flats. The trash can outside serves as a refrigerator for meat and butter, and there is fresh milk daily.

Breakfast alternates between fried eggs and boiled grain, milk, and maple syrup. Lionel drinks his coffee black, and his son drinks it with raw milk. Theron notices worms in his turds on the cold nights when he uses the porcelain pot beneath his bed. He says nothing to his father, feels no ill effect from the parasites, and will be given a vermifuge tablet like many of his schoolmates when he attends school for the first time next fall.

It snows every week and, some weeks, every day, all day and night. The drifting snow obscures the lower half of the first story's windows, curtailing what little light enters the farmhouse during December and January's short days. The house is, as Lionel tells his son, easier to heat with all the snow drifted over the moldy hay he forked up against the sills in the fall to keep out the frost.

For most of the long winter, Theron's left to his own devices. He can't read yet and, if he could, there are no books in his father's house, as Lionel can barely read the little mail and few town notices he gets.

Linwood Cleveland had made his son Ben a primitive set of building logs from ten-inch striped-maple branches, and Ben showed Theron how to lash verticals to an upright wall with heavy thread. They made frontier forts to stave off savage Indian attacks and large barns in which they put bound hay stalks they made from straw for their imaginary livestock. Linwood also made the boys whistles. The bark of striped maple, or whistle wood, as it was also known, could be loosened and slid off the cambium with ease and, by cutting away half the inner wood lengthwise, making a notch in the front, and sliding the bark back on, one could make a whistle or even a flute if one were musically inclined.

Theron still has his whistle and, over a lonely summer, gathers several dozen branches of the versatile wood and whittles them to length with his father's buck knife. Alone in his room, he often replicates the projects he and Ben built together. During one of his rambles in the woods alone, he finds pieces of a fox skeleton that he pockets and brings back to his room along with two recently shed snakeskins.

From a crumbling shale outcrop, Theron gathers a number of small rectangular pieces from which he erects small stone farm buildings. These, along with his collection of feathers, are his toys. He owns no store-bought toys.

Each year one of his former foster siblings received a real toy, starting with the oldest, then advancing annually to younger brothers and sisters. Outgrown toys could be handed down. Buying only one Christmas toy allowed Linwood and Emma to buy durable and useful items from which all the siblings might take some joy. Theron can't imagine being given such a toy, as his father goes to town to trade only for flour, sugar, and coffee, and sometimes nails. Theron doesn't see the pints of fruit-flavored brandy stashed away in the barn.

The winter is unrelenting, and by mid-March, Lionel and his son have burned five cords of dry wood. Next year's green wood lies in a heap under several feet of snow beside the barn, waiting to be stacked and dried this spring, as a green log added to a bed of hot coals only smolders and hisses steam, producing almost no heat. Early March sees temperatures oscillating between just above zero by midafternoon to thirty below just before dawn. This continues for ten days straight.

As if by intuition, Lionel's younger brother Adrian arrives in a borrowed buckboard the day after his brother burns the last of his dry wood. The temperature in the uninsulated house is falling rapidly, but it's still above freezing in the kitchen. Adrian has followed an Elmore Township horse-drawn snow roller, compacting the most recent snowfall. When he reaches his brother's rusty mailbox, familiar because it is gripped firmly in the jaws of a disused bear trap, he pulls as far off the narrow road as he can. He shouts a couple of times until Lionel shows up at the side of the road in a pair of bear-paw snowshoes. After a terse greeting, the brothers decide the three will have to shovel an area wide enough for Adrian to pull entirely off the road so they can unload the quarter cord of dry sugar maple into a pile halfway between the road and the house. The wood is a lifesaver for Lionel and his son. Lionel is usually prepared for life's emergencies, but the winter's persistent low temperatures and heavy snowfalls have caught him off guard.

By 3:15 the light is fading and there's enough space to get the buckboard off the road. Theron leads

Adrian's horse into the barn, where he shares hay with the cows. The three have been shoveling for two hours. They'll carry in enough wood for the night and unload the rest in the morning. When they finally head indoors, it's dark. The house offers shelter from the wind, but no real relief from the cold.

Lionel puts a handful of tinder in the stove, laying small sticks and branches at angles around it. He lights the small tepee, and when it's burning well he adds three small splits, two on the coals, and one in the middle to draw. Soon shards of light outline the cookstove's joints. But heat comes more slowly than light; it'll be another hour before the Glenwood shares its warmth.

By six o'clock it's comfortable in the kitchen. It'll take the rest of the night for the Glenwood to infuse the upstairs with its warmth, as heat billows up through the cast-iron floor grates to the cold floor above. It's no mystery why country dwellers live in their kitchens and sleep upstairs under heavy quilts. Living rooms and parlors are only for the few summer months.

Lionel pours himself and his brother a brandy. Theron doesn't see his father having two or three jelly jars of brandy for each one that his uncle nurses. He knows his uncle only by reputation. He's heard him called "eccentric" and a "loner."

"How's this 'ere young hellcat doin'? Takin' after 'is mother, or 'is no-good father?"

"'Ave to ask him," mutters Lionel.

"Well, son, which is it? You more like yer ma or yer pappy?"

"I dunno sir, never knew my ma. Did you know 'er?"

"She was as good as you could imagine, boy. Smart and beautiful, more than my brother ever deserved, promise ya that!" Adrian answers goodheartedly.

"What color was her hair? Did she smile a lot?" Theron asks.

"'Nough a' this fer now. She died givin' birth to you, don'cha know? She'd be here today if it wa'n't for that," Lionel mutters.

Theron's has not heard this before and fails to understand how his birth could have killed his mother. No one has explained this to him, but his father's sullen reminder silences him. Theron sits quietly at the table, pretending to busy himself with a salt shaker. Uncle Adrian breaks the loud silence, saying to his nephew, "I lost my woman as well. Girlfriend Lizzy went lickety-split on me and moved up north to some island in the Saint Lawrence with some woman she met in Grange—*Boston marriage*, p'lite folk calls it. Don' miss her none, but she was a looker."

"'Nough a' this talk," Lionel interrupts. "The boy's just turned six and don' need ta know about such all."

"Heed your own mouth, then," shoots back

Adrian. "Ain' his fault Thelma died birthin' 'im. Don't lay that on 'im. We all got 'nough trouble in life without haulin' that stone around."

Theron leaves the kitchen for the cool upstairs and crawls into bed hungry. The cold quilt on his bed draws warmth from his own small body, and his hunger remains. He falls asleep listening to his father and uncle bellowing at one another like two old bulls.

Before midnight Theron feels a tap on his shoulder. It's his uncle Adrian holding out a mug of stew with a spoon in it. "Eat some a' this and then go back ta sleep. You'll sleep better. I brought a pot of it for us all. I know why you went to bed. Don't fret. Your pa just drank too much. He din't mean nothin' by what he said about your ma. She misses you up in heaven. Now eat this and go back ta sleep. She'll come to you in your dreaming."

With that, his uncle leaves the door ajar. Theron sits up and spoons up the warm stew. It reminds him of meals from his days with the Clevelands, and soon he's asleep again, the empty mug on the floor beside the iron bedpost and the porcelain bed pot.

6

EARLY THAT SPRING, THERON FINDS MAGS. THE kitten appears to be his litter's sole survivor in a cellar hole where Theron often goes to watch milk snakes warming their cold blood amid the foundation rubble. He hears a faint mewling from beneath a section of collapsed plaster and wall studs. Eyeing the snakes warily, he picks his way down to find the source of the noise. Pulling apart the wreckage, he discovers a tiger kitten with extra toes blinking up into the sunlight. He buttons the tiny furball into his shirt, climbs out of the ruins, and walks the quarter mile home to show his dad and to ask him how to save its tiny life.

With his hard hands, Lionel gently lifts his son's discovery to his chest, peers at it and says, "Last thing we need here's another mouth to feed, but I don't 'spect he'll eat all that much." Pulling the handkerchief from his back overall pocket, he dips a corner into the pitcher of warm milk still on the dining room table from their breakfast coffee, then presses it against the lips of the kitten sitting in his other hand. The kitten eagerly sucks the corner into his mouth and nurses.

"Here," Lionel says to his son, "I gots chores. You do this 'til he's full up and falls asleep, then set

'im over there in my chair. He'll be fine. You'll need
to feed him like I done ever' hour or so 'til he comes
back full to life. Tyke's probably been 'lone for some
time and lucky he din't get et by whatever et th' rest
of his fambly. I'll be in the upper meadow. I'll need
your help this afternoon scrumpin' apple drops for
the pigs."

Summer comes late, and Theron spends every
waking moment outside with Mags trotting alongside
him. He helps his father with chores when asked, and
routine chores he does without being reminded. These
include unpegging the oak barn stanchions after his
father's done the morning milking and leading "the
girls" out to one of the two pastures for grazing. He's
responsible for counting them as they pass through the
gate; the count must always be twenty-one.

Theron has whittled his own cow prod, a birch
whip taller than he is. He uses it only to keep the girls
moving. It's light and doesn't hurt them, only reminding them to keep moving along; even creatures of habit
can sometimes be forgetful.

When the ground is firm again after drying out
from the spring thaw, Theron and his dad stack wood
inside the ell extending off the kitchen's back door.
Lionel loads wood into a wooden wheelbarrow with
a cast-iron wheel, brings it inside, and dumps it near
where Theron stacks. The father has tutored the son

on how to crisscross chunks at each end of the pile to support its horizontal pressure and how to rock and settle each log carefully into the pile. Theron likes the work; he soon learns to eye specific chunks that mesh with gaps in the steadily-rising pile. And once it's over his head, he begins another row. Each time Lionel dumps another wheelbarrow of logs by the pile he looks over his son's work, sometimes making a suggestion or resettling a chunk, but generally expressing satisfaction. Mags keeps an eye out for mice skittering out of the pile.

At noon they break for a lunch of cold boiled carrots and potatoes they dip in a coffee can of bacon fat. They pocket some mushy overwintered apples and go back to work. Later, when they take a break, they'll wash them down with cups of leftover morning coffee. Theron likes the taste of coffee, but only with lots of milk.

Theron is responsible for the biddies. Every morning he opens the small henhouse door and counts as each of the sixteen hens pokes a suspicious head through the opening and scans the yard with her beady eyes for danger. Satisfied, she picks her way carefully down the dry-rotted board to the ground where she will begin a daylong scrabble for worms and bugs. When the last one has landed and the yard is dotted with biddies, the rooster sticks his head out, surveys his harem, and then goosesteps grandly down to join them. If it's rained during the night and the rotting walkway is slippery, the biddies and rooster slip and slide down the ramp into a feathery heap at the bottom. This always makes Theron laugh.

After dusk the biddies all return on their own and Theron goes in through the large door with a lantern to count and see that all sixteen hens and the rooster are perched high above him on the maple whip that hangs over his head from the coop's rafters or in their nests. He gathers eggs in a wire basket, checks their water, latches the henhouse door, returns to the house, and reports his egg and biddy count to his father if he is there. Most of all, Theron loves reaching under a hen's downy warmth to lift out her clutch of eggs and put them, still warm, into his basket. One evening Theron asks his father how eggs come to be, and Lionel gives a succinct explanation of how and why hens lay eggs. The explanation elicits questions but, sensing his father's mood, Theron withholds them.

Occasionally a hen will go broody and sit for days on a pile of eggs or, sometimes, on no eggs at all. His father has taught him to lift her out of her nesting box and carry her outside with the others.

Without saying anything to his father, he decides to leave a buff hen on her eggs to see what happens. Lionel only sets foot in the henhouse a few times a year, when the two must clean out the stalagmites of shit that rise under the perch high above. In the evening, when Theron goes in to collect the eggs and count the flock, he stops to watch the nesting hen, who eyes him suspiciously. Occasionally he catches her off her five eggs, drinking some water or pecking at the corn and kitchen scraps he leaves for her in a shallow tin. When she returns, he watches her rearrange her eggs in the nest, rolling them slightly. She then settles herself on them again and fluffs her feathers out to be sure her eggs are all snug underneath her.

Later that summer, their efforts shift to cutting wood for the coming winter. Lionel fells and limbs trees up to a foot wide with a double-headed axe, while Theron gathers limbs and branches into a pile nearby. His job is to cut the limbs into firewood and kindling with a bucksaw. He lays a branch across the sawbuck and, using a measuring sample his father cut to sixteen inches, draws the crosscut saw back and forth until the overhanging piece falls to the ground. He learns not to apply downward pressure and bind the saw, but to let the teeth his father sharpens regularly do their work. These pieces he gathers up, aligns, and ties into manageable bundles with twine to carry back to the shed. When Theron is his father's age, he'll remember what he's learned from his father about gathering and curing firewood and the warmth it imparts on long winter nights.

Theron accompanies his father doing chores, watching to learn for later on, and being available for those he can manage now, like emptying the milk bucket through a felt filter into the ten-gallon, tinned milk cans, though he's not yet strong enough to move the cans themselves. He accompanies his father when he mucks out gutters and helps shovel fresh manure into the wheelbarrow with a square-end shovel. When the wheelbarrow's full, his father wheels it out a corner door of the barn onto a rickety plank trestle over the manure pile and dumps it for later use in the garden, the rhubarb patch, or what Lionel calls his finishing pasture.

When not helping with chores, Theron spends his time alone in the woods with Mags. During his first summer in the Flats, the places he returns to most earn names, affix themselves in his memory, and remain there the rest of his life. His favorite spot is a glen where cold water tumbles down smooth, moss-covered boulders into a small, gravel-filled, waist-deep basin. The glen is bordered by a profusion of ostrich ferns, dewy from the moisture hanging in the air.

Later that summer, Lionel gives him a dozen barbed fish hooks and a reel of fishing line. He shows him how to tie a snell knot to secure the hook to the line, and together they fashion a primitive fishing pole out of river birch. His new pole becomes Theron's most treasured possession, and every chance he gets he heads to the glen to catch the small brookies lurking beneath the overhanging bank.

As days shorten again, Theron looks forward to the start of school, even though his knowledge of it is only anecdotal. Mostly, he looks forward to seeing other kids again. But he also sees worrisome changes in his father's behavior: small stumbles, a task forgotten, or just slurred words to someone absent as he goes about his chores. Routine chores are sometimes missed entirely, like cleaning leaves out of the spring box, refilling the kerosene lamps, or replenishing the wood bin behind the cookstove.

One evening in late August, Theron asks his dad when they'll go blackberry picking higher up the ridge. There's no answer. He asks again, and there's still no answer. He realizes his father's asleep and they've not had supper. There's a strong smell of alcohol around him. Theron recognizes this smell mostly from the glass jar of rubbing alcohol his father keeps in the barn to wipe down infected cow teats or to treat the foot fungus that plagues some of their hens; he knows his father can't drink this, as the label bears a skull and crossbones, but he's seen his father drink when Uncle Adrian comes by, and he suspects he is drinking more—or using less guile to hide it. One night earlier that week he had watched as his father uncorked a bottle of clear liquid from the pantry shelf with no skull and crossbones and made no bones about pouring some of it into a glass of cider.

"What chu starin' at?" Lionel had said that night.

Theron now turns and goes to his room, where he's taken to keeping a paper bag of apples and carrots for the nights when his father's too drunk to make supper. He lies on his bed with Mags curled up between his knees, imagining school and listening to his father's angry, half-dreaming monologue in the kitchen below.

7

WHEN ADRIAN GIVES HIS NEPHEW HIS FIRST RIFLE, a Winchester .22, he teaches him how to shoot and clean it and, after several Saturday afternoons shooting tin cans off fence posts, he takes him hunting. Theron's first kill haunts him. A rabbit sitting high on its rear haunches twenty yards away, with its head high, sniffs the air. Theron follows his uncle's whispered instructions, keeping the bead centered in the notch welded to the barrel, and slowly squeezes the trigger. The animal seems so small and far away; he doesn't expect to hit it. Theron is taken aback by the loud crack of the rifle's discharge. The rabbit leaps lopsided into the air and falls to the ground, its right hind leg clawing frantically at its upper torso, as if to fend off some invisible predator. He is shocked by what he sees, and runs up to the animal. He stands over it and watches the frantic clawing subside and the rabbit panting and looking at him with fear. Theron raises the barrel to the rabbit's head, reloads, and ends Theron's and the rabbit's misery.

In the fall, Theron's uncle Adrian spots and begins tracking a six-point buck. One Saturday he enlists

Theron to join him in the hunt, and the two pick up the track just after sunrise and follow the buck up along the mountain ridge to a hemlock thicket. Theron carries his .22, but knows he'll have to use Adrian's Model 94 .30-30 to kill a deer. Handing off the .30-30 to his nephew, Theron gets off a shot, but only wounds his target in the shoulder. The two track the bleeding buck for a half mile until it collapses, and Adrian shows his nephew how to deliver a kill shot. As with the rabbit before, Theron can't erase the look he sees in the buck's limpid eyes.

More than two decades later, when Adrian returns home from the hostilities in Belleau Wood in France, missing half an arm and adjusting to his new moniker, Stub, the deaths he's witnessed have changed him as well. He's seen an imperious race of men marching robotically around, barking orders at one another incomprehensibly. He's watched two new friends from his unit drop wordlessly next to him, and another die slowly in horrific pain, crying and begging Adrian to convey his love to people Adrian doesn't know. When the medics arrive with their morphine and push Adrian aside, his friend keeps looking at him and pleading. As the anodyne begins to camouflage the pain, Adrian's friend closes his eyes and begins talking instead to his mother, four thousand miles away.

Theron and his uncle drag the deer home on a travois they hastily fashion from two gray birch whips cross-strung with woody grapevine. They hang the carcass from the ancient sugar maple shading Theron's second-floor bedroom and dress it, Adrian describing to his nephew the cuts and how to remove the warm organs—which to keep and which to discard. The pungent smell of intestines flowing from the deer's abdominal cavity stays with Theron for several days, but it's the look in the deer's eyes when he fired the last shot that haunts his dreams. Is it terror or gratitude he sees?

8

SCHOOL IS A RELIEF TO BOTH FATHER AND SON. LIONEL can drink as he wishes, and Theron is again among those his own age.

In 1895, Elmore has seven lumber mills; eight standard schools dotting the landscape between Wolcott, Woodbury, Worcester, and Morristown; and 680 residents. The area's been heavily logged and, one by one, the seven mills are shutting down. Three cedar oil mills prosper however, as they produce the pungent oil used to coat and protect the industrial machinery being fabricated farther south in Windsor. The demand for cedar oil will continue to grow as a preservative for the steel weaponry soon to take such a terrible human toll in what will come to be known as the Great War.

Fifty-three hill farms sustain most Elmore families, including the few who live in the Flats. Standard School No. 244 has fourteen students in its one room, a few of whom will go on to People's Academy in Morristown when they pass their first nine grades. Others will begin full-time work on their family's farm, or will take a job logging or at one of the mills.

Lionel's day begins with a generous pour of fruit brandy or grain alcohol into his first coffee as he heads for the barn to do the morning milking. Theron helps him for an hour and a half, and then eats three hard-boiled eggs with a cup of creamy coffee and sets off at seven for school on foot.

As a young girl in Standard School No. 244, Clara Emmons always talked of becoming a teacher. Now, at the age of twenty-seven, Miss Emmons knows her charges well. She also knows their family circumstances, and tailors her curriculum and her occasional disciplines to that knowledge. She has no children of her own, nor is she married. She has heard from Elise, who is also the school nurse, of Lionel's "bibulousness," but Theron is hardly the only child growing up in a drinking household. Most households have two parents, however, and she worries that Theron has no sober person to look after him. Clara Emmons and Thelma were friends, and she feels an obligation to her dead friend to keep a special watch on her child.

Theron likes school. He learns quickly, takes his homework seriously, and handles rote and written work well. Solitude has left him with many open questions, to which answers reveal themselves as he advances year by year through the grades at his same wooden desk. Some answers come from new friends he makes; others are revealed in the studies and reading assignments he must complete to advance to the next grade. He still misses Ben, and the promise that he and Ben might meet in high school motivates his study and homework. Theron is an anxious child, and Miss Emmons works hard to satisfy his curiosity, challenge his native intelligence, and help him feel comfortable in her classroom.

Lionel is not as well-schooled as his son, having dropped out of high school to work, but he is supportive of the time Theron spends in school. When he's sober enough to notice his son reading the *McGuffey Reader* at the dining room table in the jaundiced halo of a greasy oil lamp, he experiences a brief moment of pride.

Theron worries about his father, and Miss Emmons worries about Theron. The school is two and a half miles from Lionel's farmhouse and sits at the corner where Flats Road veers off from Woodbury Road.

For Miss Emmons, a barometer of her students' well-being is what they do during recess; even in the most inclement weather, she accompanies them outside and monitors their activity. She is accountable for their well-being indoors and out and, unlike some of her colleagues, has no classroom assistant. She likes to watch the boys roughhousing and playing King of the Hill in winter on the nearby snowbank. She sees in their behavior the natural clamoring for hierarchy so typical in boys, and she knows the energy they expend fighting one another to occupy the summit will not be used to disrupt her classroom later. Theron engages with the boys his age, but doesn't show the competitive energy that some display in their rough-and-tumble games.

The girls cluster under an eave or beneath the flourishing elm that shelters much of the playground, whispering furtively to one another and occasionally pointing at the boys, showing disdain for their juvenile behavior. They're thankful to be more mature and above such childishness. Though they're just discovering it, the insouciance they display on the playground betrays their advancing physical development, but they must be patient and wait for the rowdy boys playing by themselves to catch up and begin noticing them.

9

MISS EMMONS, ELISE, UNCLE ADRIAN, AND Leonard have all seen to it that Theron has adequate winter clothing; they're hand-me-downs, but they still offer warmth in the coldest weather.

By sixth grade Theron is used to coming home to an empty house with no supper. He sets off from school in the waning light and arrives home after dark. Knowing what awaits him at home, Miss Emmons sometimes invents a pretext to have Theron stay after school to help her with chores or to preview a book she's chosen for him from the Elmore library. His curiosity about physics, natural phenomena, and machines makes it easy for her to choose books or periodicals that he'll finding interesting. With the other children gone, she can also bring out the extra sandwich she often packs for him in her tin lunchbox.

One night in January, Theron is walking home along Flats Road. The road is clear, as it's been too cold to snow. It usually takes him forty minutes to walk the two and a half miles home unless the weather's bad. Then it can take an hour or more.

It's dark by four o'clock, and when he reaches the stand of white birches along the road marking the north boundary of their property, he's surprised not to see a light burning in either the house or the barn. Lionel usually finishes the evening milking and feeding before he falls comatose into his hickory rocker by the woodstove, where Theron usually finds him after the long walk home. This night, however, Lionel's nowhere to be seen. As usual, the buckboard's sitting next to the chicken coop, so he knows his father's home. Theron can tell the fire's been out for some time, as it's cold in the kitchen and the stove is cold to the touch.

Theron runs to the barn and fumbles in the dark for the mason jar of stick matches to light the lantern hanging on a nail nearby. Lionel is careful to keep such an essential tool in a consistent place so it can be found in the dark.

Theron turns up the wick, and the burning kerosene infuses the area around him with a pale yellow light. He doesn't see his father, and begins to worry that he might be hurt or have stumbled in the woods, lying outside unable to call out or to make his way to the house or barn. He walks along the gutter way, surveying the cows to see if they've been milked. They stand quiet in the shadows, which they wouldn't do had his father not completed the afternoon milking. At the far end, Theron sees Edna lying down and walks back to see if she's okay. Edna's freshened every year for the last seven years, producing healthy young calves, and only one bull calf in that time. She's earned the privilege of not being stanchioned at night.

Theron approaches carefully and holds up the lantern to see if she's all right. Edna lifts her head slightly, looking up into the light. Theron sees his father passed out and lying huddled against her haunches. He's moved in as close as he can to Edna's underbelly to take advantage of her warmth.

Tears begin to well up in Theron's eyes. "Dad . . . Dad . . . Get up. It's freezing, and we gotta get in the house."

Lionel doesn't respond. Theron sees with relief the rise and fall of his father's chest and yells again at him to get up. The loud sound causes Edna to scramble to her feet, and Lionel's head, nestled in her haunch, flops back onto the concrete pad with an audible thump. Theron pulls his father out from under the standing cow, away from her hooves, and onto the walkway behind the gutter.

"Dad . . . Please, please, Dad, get up. I can't carry you to the house. Get up Dad—please get up." His father lies unresponsive on the concrete.

Theron runs back into the house to light a fire in the stove, knowing it'll be three hours before the house begins to warm. He takes the woolen sleigh blanket from his father's bed and carries it back to the barn, hoping to wrap his father in it until he can wake him and coerce him into the house. He lays the blanket next to his father, who's making gurgling noises, and wraps the blanket around him, tucking the edge under him. He returns to the house to restoke the fire, filling the Glenwood's small firebox with biscuit wood to coax out the most heat.

Theron eats some raw oats with milk and returns to the barn. He finds his father wrapped in the blanket and sitting against the white-washed barn wall.

"Git," his father growls. "Git up the 'ouse. I won' be 'long. Jes' got tired 'n' fell ta sleep. Git 'long and do yer 'omeworks."

Theron looks at his father. "You're drunk and don't preten' ya ain't. I ain't pretendin' any longer."

With that he turns and runs back to the house.

10

I N 1902 LIONEL'S YOUNGER BROTHER ADRIAN GRAD-uates from the Johnson Normal School fourteen miles away. A training academy for educators, Johnson is the first step toward fulfilling Adrian's childhood dream of being a teacher.

Unlike Lionel, Adrian excelled in grade school and later at People's Academy. Logging and farming held little interest, although he loved the outdoors and worked hard at the several part-time and summer jobs that sustained him during his studies.

After graduation he's offered a job at his alma mater in Morristown and begins the fall after graduation, teaching English grammar and world history.

Adrian boards with the Morton family, which owns the local hardware and lumber store. He loves to lie in his second-floor dormer room with its saggy iron-frame bed and read late into the night. He's always been an avid reader, reading across cultures and centuries and spending any spare time trolling the shelves of the tiny Carnegie Library in Morristown for books of interest. He's particularly intrigued by the evolution and diversity of spoken English, and often visits the reference shelf to understand colloquialisms, idioms, and arcane words he's never encountered. Having completed two years of Latin in high school, he's particularly fond of the Latinate English words he encounters and can decipher from their component Latin syllables. He had considered becoming a Latin teacher, but worried that teaching a single language might, over time, be limiting. Perhaps it was the stern pedagogy of Madge Churchill, under whose eagle eye he learned to diagram English sentences on a blackboard, that made Latin's rigid rules come so easily to him. He found the visual architecture of a deconstructed sentence more enlightening than the endless rote rules in his grammar text.

This study of English usage heightens Adrian's awareness of how his own friends and neighbors talk to him and one another. He becomes a fan of the occasional malapropisms he overhears among rurals, whose oratorical pretenses belie their early retirement from the educational system.

One day after his first year of teaching, he's visited by Elise, the township's visiting and school nurse. He's seen her around school, but knows her mostly as an informal guardian of his nephew Theron, only twelve years his junior.

Sitting on a bench with Adrian by the cannon in the park, Elise confides her fears about his older brother's excessive drinking and his nephew's general welfare. Theron's teacher, Clara Emmons, has conveyed to Elise her concerns about the household in which Theron is growing up: the lack of proper meals, the hard work at odd hours, and the times Theron comes late to school because he's had to stay home and milk the cows when his father fails to get out of bed.

Adrian also worries about his brother and nephew living alone together in the middle of nowhere, with no neighbors and only a swaybacked Belgian and ancient buckboard for transport. Although his studies have occupied his time and focus, he's not forgotten all that's left of his family. He promises Elise to visit the Flats more often and asks her to let Miss Emmons know she can call on him at any time if she's worried. He thanks Elise for her concern and lopes down to Peck's for a coffee and a piece of mincemeat pie.

11

THE FOLLOWING SATURDAY ADRIAN HARNESSES UP
Ajax to the Mortons' buggy and heads toward
the Flats. The winter sun shimmers over a light new
snowfall, the bright landscape broken only by the
skeletons of deciduous trees. Adrian pulls his visored
hat down over his forehead to shade the glare and see
where he's going, but Ajax knows the way and Adrian
is free to scan the landscape as they head past Elmore
Mountain and the lake. Some locals have shoveled off
a quarter acre behind the Elmore general store, and a
few couples skate blissfully there.

Adrian knows his brother is defensive about his
drinking and resentful of being reminded that others
are aware of it. Alcoholism is no stranger to this clois-
tered community, but it is rarely discussed unless a
drinker makes a public display of him- or herself or
injures someone as a result of drunkenness. No support groups exist in which to dry out; ministers coun-
sel the tosspots among their flocks, the school
principal disciplines boys caught sneaking alcohol on
or near the school grounds and threatens them with
confinement in the Weeks School a hundred miles
away in Vergennes, and Officer McMahon handles

cases where alcohol consumption has led to a destructive spree, casualty, or theft. Hardened drunks are involuntarily committed to the Waterbury State Hospital for the Insane, which has only just opened twenty miles away. Lurid tales from those unfortunate enough to have undergone treatment for drunkenness there ought to induce abstinence but, sadly, alcohol overwhelms reason and even love for most drinkers.

Lionel's self-exile in the Flats and his son's fear and embarrassment for his father camouflage their pain to all except the few keeping watch. Lionel is not abusive, and the one time his son confronted him splayed on the barn floor in incoherent drunkenness, Theron was not punished physically but endured four days of angry silence and a sad look of betrayal in his father's eyes.

Theron greets his Uncle Adrian with excitement; a visitor relieves him of his need to manage, if not parent, his father. Theron's beginning his final year at the standard school, and he hopes to attend People's Academy next year and board in town during the week. He still dreams of finding Ben there, although they have not seen each other now for ten years. His father meets the animated conversation between his brother and his son with a mute sense of betrayal. Like smoke from an untended fire in the woodstove, years of abandoned conversations hang heavy in their kitchen.

Theron knows Uncle Adrian can never be intimidated by his older brother. Adrian greets anger with humor and self-pity with scorn. He once explained to his nephew that no one's anger at Lionel's behavior can ever match the anger Lionel must feel toward himself. The paradox eluded Theron at the time, but later it comes to make sense.

After that first visit, Adrian comes more regularly, on weekend mornings when he hopes his brother will be sober. But Lionel's sobriety is now relative, as his hangovers and binges merge.

It's early March 1904, and time to tap the sugar maples that lie on the south edge of the pasture. There are no delineated property boundaries and no one, save the Elmore town clerk, has much of an idea who owns what or where it lies. The vast resources of the Flats are open to the few inhabitants industrious enough to harvest them: game, firewood, cedar oil, shang, and maple syrup.

The size of Lionel's sugar works is limited to the number of rusty buckets he still has. He's managed to repair a few with river bottom clay, but the sap often loosens the clay and he loses the sap and the bucket. A pile of old buckets sits next to the woodpile inside the shed. Lionel has no sledge, just an old toboggan his grandfather made from white oak slats bent and shaped over a steaming syrup kettle. Theron and

Adrian pile the usable buckets and a small sack of spile taps on the toboggan. Theron goes to the house to get the makings of coffee: the enamel pot, three tin cups, a small jar of last year's maple syrup, and a cheese-cloth full of yesterday's damp coffee grounds. Lionel gathers a boring auger and wood mallet from the shelf, and the three head off into a nearby covert of mature maples. The sky is cloudless, and a winter sun warms the air.

Adrian bores new holes or reams old ones with the auger, and Lionel hammers in spiles with the mal-let, while Theron fetches a bucket and secures it to the spile. Sometime after noon they break for coffee. Theron has been charged with building a fire and cut-ting a tripod of alders to hang the coffeepot from. He fills the pot from a nearby creek, and soon steam's emerging from the spout.

"Yest'day's grounds gonna need more boilin'," observes Lionel.

Theron hands out the cups and makes the rounds, holding the hot handle with the double-folded flap of his flannel shirt as he fills each mug with coffee. He then passes the maple syrup to Adrian, who keeps it moving around the small circle. Uncle and son see Lionel pour a clear liquid into his coffee.

Sensing their disapproval, Lionel mutters, "Don't s'pose y'all wan' any hooch? Warm ya up and give ya 'durance."

Neither son nor uncle acknowledge the question. "No need ta take offense, jes' askin.'"

"None taken," answers Adrian. "Keep 'at up and we'll 'ave to have ya declared mentally incontinent."

Adrian is the only one to laugh at his joke.

With sixty-seven maples tapped, the trio heads home. The light is fading, and Adrian sees his brother stumbling over his bearpaw snowshoes.

At home Theron feeds the woodstove and refills the woodbin from the shed before hanging up his winter coat. Father and uncle are seated at the table with two mason jars of applejack distilled by a neighbor deeper in the Flats.

"Wha' ya teachin' at that school a yourn?" asks Lionel.

"English grammar, history, study hall, and recess. I get one free period a day."

"All head work, no hard work?"

"I sometimes teach the boys ta wrassle during recess. Keeps 'em from hurtin' one another. I like my work. I'm one of the few man teachers. Most are elderly teacher-biddies, been there for a century or more. Good teachers, mind ya, tough as nails. Some'r widder-ladies and two of 'em are in a Boston marriage—great girls, very discreet and good with the roughest cases."

"So you th' only man teacher in a school full a' wimmens?"

"No, Red Herring, the principal, teaches shop and algebra when he's not takin' his so-called board of education—the paddle he made in shop and keeps by his desk—to some young rascal's behind. His real name's Red Fancher, always looks like his hair's on fire from being so red. We call him Red Herring 'cause his principaling never makes much sense. But not many of the teacher-biddies pay much attention to 'im. The boys do, though, 'cause he enjoys more 'en he should whackin' 'em with that board of education. Keeps 'em in line for the most part."

"Theron, here, wants to go to your school but I need 'em here to t' help me wi' chores 'n' all and, sides, how's 'e gonna make a six-mile trip twice a day. Can't spare 'im for five days in town. Things gotta get done 'ere, and I can't do 'em all by my lonesome," Lionel mutters, staring at a burnt ring in the oak table.

"One of the teachers, Connie Boyce, lives in Elmore and drives back and forth each day. I could move in with you two, keep some order here, and help out on weekends, and Theron 'n' I could ride to school together with Connie. I'd pay her a li'l somethin' for the pleasure of our comp'ny."

Lionel's silence conveys his displeasure.

"Well, you think on it. You got a bright son 'ere needs learnin'. Don't want 'im to end up an ol' weasel-dick like you at twenty-nine. I'll be back next week, and we'll figure on it then. Meanwhile, Theron, you keep yer chin up and yer fly buttoned. Help your pa, and keep yer nose in the books if ya wanna go anywhere." Adrian dons his woolen jacket and heads out, pulling the door shut firmly behind him.

"Ya hungry, Dad?" Theron asks to break the loaded silence. "I can make some buttered turnips or potatoes for us."

"I ain' hungry. Suit yerself," Lionel responds, pouring himself more applejack from a blue-tinted jar.

Theron peels and boils three potatoes for himself, mashing them up with some salt and butter when they become soft. He pours himself some milk, fills a saucer for Mags, and takes the warm pot of potatoes up to his cool room.

Sitting on his bed with Mags curled up next to him, Theron is sleepy from the hard work. Having Adrian visit is a relief, but Theron's still anxious knowing that his father will drink himself to sleep again. He worries that Lionel will fail to get up, and that he'll be two hours late to school for having to milk the girls in his father's stead. At least he and Mags will be alone until the sun or their rooster wakes him for school.

12

L ATER IN MARCH, THERON HEADS OUT IN SNOW-shoes to check the sap buckets and finds them mostly full. A few have lost their clay patches and hang empty, but there's a bountiful harvest. He's hoping his father can again borrow Neal Slater's sledge and collecting tank to gather the sap and bring it back for spring boiling as they have in the past. Theron stands under a century-old maple. Its trunk is a good forty inches in diameter. The sun's high in a blue sky, and Theron's standing in a shower of sap leaking from broken branches higher up in the ancient tree. He can smell maple and moves aside only when the gentle rain of sap begins to soak through his flannel shirt. He heads home to give his father the good news about the maple crop and to remind him to ask Mr. Slater about borrowing his sledge.

There's a lively fire in the cookstove. His father must be in the barn doing a late milking. Theron unstraps his snowshoes, hangs them on the peg, and heads down the path to the barn. As he approaches, however, he hears the cows complaining about not having been milked. Late-day spring light lingers in the sky, but it's well after five and they're used to being milked at four. Theron calls for his dad, but hears no answer. He walks along the gutter and again finds his father curled up against Edna's haunches. He's conscious this time, and Theron hears him talking quietly to the Guernsey as if she were a person. Lionel doesn't sense his son's presence. Theron remains still.

"Miss her ever' day, don'cha know. She was my tenderness, and there ain' been none in my life since she died birthin' the young'un. Don' ever see any other wimmens, don' wanna, neither. Thelma knew how to tender me. Hard, too, raisin' a boy by m'self. Done 'e best I could, but 'e'd be better off with Adrian 'n' wi' me. Dunno, though, if I could live out 'ere by my lonesome, carin' for you and the girls, haulin' milk cans and firewood 'n' all. Wish Thelma's here with me. Still miss 'er ever' day."

Edna chews her cud, oblivious to Lionel's monologue. Theron knows he'll have to milk and make supper. He leaves his father with Edna and begins the milking.

Well after sunset, Theron climbs the path to the house and is struck by the blaze of color still in the western sky. He finds his father slumped in his chair. He fries up two pieces of venison steak, eats one, cuts up some small pieces for Mags, and leaves the other on the edge of the stove for his father when—or *if*—he wakes up. He throws three splits in the stove and climbs the stairs to bed.

Theron hasn't written the essay on President Lincoln's early years assigned for tomorrow. He's read the material, but hasn't started the essay. He knows Miss Emmons will understand, but he wishes he could just hand her the finished report on time like most of the kids in class. He wishes she'd get angry at him and dock his grade when he turns in papers late. Everyone's kindness and understanding inhibits his own anger. He has two study halls tomorrow, and will try to finish the assignment before school lets out.

13

As THERON'S LAST YEAR AT STANDARD SCHOOL NO.
244 winds down, Miss Emmons approaches him
during recess and asks if he's going to People's in the
fall. Theron demurs, looking at his shoes in silence;
she's asking him about a decision over which he feels
he has no control. Miss Emmons persists, telling him
he must go on and get his high school degree. She tells
him his mother would want him to finish high school,
but this maternal allusion elicits nothing. Theron
never knew his mother and, apart from the kindness
of Emma Cleveland, Elise, and Miss Emmons, Theron's
never known anything like a mother's care and tenderness. Having parented an alcoholic father for most
of his own childhood, he sometimes thinks about how
much he envied Emma Cleveland's open displays of
affection for her own children.

Over the weekend, Miss Emmons again consults
Adrian, and the two agree that Theron must go on to
high school. Adrian explains his plan to move in with
his brother and commute from Elmore with Connie
Boyce, even though he knows the plan won't work.
It's a half-hour walk each way to and from Connie's
house on Route 12, and Adrian knows he can't claim

weather as an excuse for leaving a class full of kids by themselves. He promises Miss Emmons to "put on his thinking cap" and come up with a workable plan. She understands his dilemma and thanks him, reminding him of her friendship with his sister-in-law and the sense of responsibility she feels for his nephew.

Adrian asks his landlady, Mrs. Morton, if Theron can stay in his room during the week for a bit more rent. Knowing the situation, she's supportive and offers to bring down a cot from the attic. "It'll be cramped, but toasty. Don't snore, do ya?" she adds with an impish smile. "Theron can count on a hearty breakfast as well, though you two'll be on your own for dinner, mind you." Adrian thanks Mrs. Morton for her understanding and generosity and puts his mind to selling the plan to his brother.

Although he's concerned about his brother's welfare, Adrian also worries about the girls. If not milked on schedule, dairy cows develop painful mastitis and die. He worries, too, about Lionel's draft horse, Luther, still working at age twenty but limping badly, still draws a buckboard full of milk cans twice a week to Route 12, hauls Neal Slater's borrowed sledge through the woods during sugaring, and skids logs in winter.

Adrian also knows that farmers whose children decline to take up the rigors of a farming life often sell out after forty or fifty years, never having had a day off, while childless farmers, unable to raise their own labor, take on hired hands—usually homeless folk or widowers working for room, board, and pocket change.

The following weekend, worried about what he might find, Adrian heads out to see his brother. There's no one home, and Luther's not in the barn. He assumes Theron and Lionel are gathering sap. He straps on a pair of snowshoes and trudges off to the sugar works. Soon he picks up the sledge's trail in the wet snow and follows it another few hundred yards into a thicket of maples. He hears Luther snorting up ahead, and spots a glint off the galvanized tin tank through the trees. Theron's lugging overflowing sap buckets to his father, who stands on the sledge runner, emptying the buckets into the tank and tossing them back down to his son. Luther snorts his impatience at being made to wait.

"'Nother twenty buckets or so and we gotta head home and unload Neal's tank inta ours," Lionel shouts.

Adrian greets the two, pitching in. Lionel nods to his brother, and Theron acknowledges his uncle with relief. After a half hour, Lionel tells the bucket runners the tank's full and the three head home with Luther limping and straining at his traces.

Lionel's lost count of the buckets, but the eight-hundred-gallon tank is almost full, and that will boil down to twenty gallons of rich syrup. He can trade fourteen gallons at the store for staples and keep six for next year.

Luther hauls the sledge up behind the barn. Lionel sends Theron to fetch a tin sluice they use to drain the sap from the tank's spigot down into the rusty tank Neal gave Lionel when he bought a new one. It's the same size, and the sap will just fill the rusty one sitting in a corner of the barn. When it's full, they'll cover it with an old linen sheet until they begin boiling next week. Lionel can't afford one of the new English tin evaporators at Morton's Hardware and still boils his sap in a sand-cast kettle he inherited from his father.

Lionel returns Neal's sledge and then walks Luther back to the barn, where he unhitches the horse collar, whiffletree, and traces and leads him into his box stall. With cupped hands he feeds Luther oats from the grain box and then gently rubs his muzzle as the old horse chews his treat. He whispers inaudibly to Luther and then takes the lantern and leaves for the house.

Adrian and Theron have stoked the woodstove. An iron pan is sizzling some bacon slabs and a dozen eggs for supper. Lionel fetches a bottle from the pantry and offers a pour to his brother. Adrian declines but watches as his brother pours half a glass of fresh sap from the day's harvest into a quart mason jar and fills the rest with applejack. Lionel drops into his chair and thanks his brother for his help. "Y'earned yer quart jar from when I'm done boilin' nex' week."

Adrian thanks his brother for the gift and steels himself for the discussion of his nephew's plans for the fall. Theron plates the bacon and eggs and adds slices from the bakery bread Adrian brought from town. The three consume the fry pan's contents together, making small talk about the day's events, and wiping their ironstone plates clean with the slices of bread. Theron and his uncle wash down their supper with cold raw milk that leaves a rich ring of butterfat around the rim of their glasses. Lionel drinks his colorless sap and applejack as if it's water.

Sensing a change in the kitchen weather, Theron rises and clears the table, pouring some boiling water from the kettle over the dishes, flatware, and glasses, then washes and dries them. Saying a quiet goodnight, he goes up to his room, where Mags is already nestled at the foot of his bed waiting for him. He sets the lantern on his bedstead, picks up the tiger cat, and scratches his forehead and back, as Mags expects him to do.

He knows Adrian will spend the night, as it's too late to begin the long journey back to town. He pulls the quilt up to his chin, waiting for his body heat to warm the bedclothes. Mags curls up near his elbow and starts purring, and the sound has a calming effect.

Uncle Adrian has brought him a library book, as he always does, and Theron begins reading *The Red Badge of Courage*. Theron studied the Civil War in history class at school and remembers Miss Emmons recalling all the families she knew in town who lost a father, son, or brother in the conflict. Their study of the war, however, is an outline of battles and dates, generals and towns, and never evokes the battlefield horror that unfolds in the book he now reads.

After he's fallen asleep, loud voices in the kitchen below make their way into his dream of swimming with Becky Shank on the far side of Lake Elmore where there are only a few houses. The discord resolves itself as he recognizes his father's slurred shouts; the image of Becky swimming next to him dissipates. Theron doesn't stir, but is fully awake now, grateful only that his father is talking with another person, not to himself, as so often happens late at night.

14

"IF'N YOU'D LOS' TH' ONLY WOMAN Y'EVER LOVED, you'd drink 'casional, too. Y'ain' ever married like I done. She died birthin' Theron, an' I lost th' only sweetness in ma goddam life."

"If y'ever blame your son in front of me for his mother's death again, I swear I'll beat the tar outta ya," Adrian fires back. "Wasn't his fault at all . . . just bein' born was all, natural as could be. Something broke inside of Thelma and she bled to death. You been 'ome and taken 'er to the Copley, she wouldn't a' bled to death, neither. Yer as much to blame as Theron for her dying. You feelin' guilty, now? Maybe you know how yer son feels most 'a his life. Women die in childbirth all the time.

"Theron don' talk much but he does well in school. Just 'cause he doesn't 'ave much ta say ta you, he still obeys ya and does your work for ya when you're drunk—which, by-the-by, is most of the time now. You better watch yerself or you'll end up droolin' and mutterin' down in Waterbury with the other wet-brain drunks."

Theron hears a chair tip over and furniture banging.

"Go ta bed, fer Chris-sake. Yer too drunk ta even fight!" Adrian shouts.

The house is finally quiet except for the sound of Adrian climbing the stairs to take the wool blanket from the adjacent room and head back down to the couch. Theron wonders if he should go down to see if everyone's all right, but he can't bring himself to leave his warm bed, and knows Adrian would neither hurt his brother nor leave him alone if he was hurt. He pulls Mags closer to him.

Adrian wakes him early the next morning. "Come on, let's milk while your dad sleeps it off. If he remembers last night, he's either gonna be angry or pouting. I already lit the stove and put on the coffee."

Theron gets up, dresses, and goes downstairs to splash cold water on his face. The water running in the spigot reminds him to pee, and he steps out on the front porch in his wool socks and pisses off the side, as he's seen his father and uncle do many times.

"You tryin' to 'tract the ladies or scare off the critters?" Adrian says with a chuckle. "You'll be needin' more'n that t' excite the ladies. Don't be rushin' it. Yer time'll come, soon enough."

The air outside is warming fast in the morning sun. Icicles drip from the eaves and the sound of moving water can be heard from the nearby creek. With two at it, milking takes a little over an hour and a bit more to pour the full pails through the felt filter into the large tinned milk cans and haul them on a toboggan up to the spring house. When Adrian and Theron return to the house, Lionel's still in his chair under his quilt where Adrian left him the night before. Adrian refills their coffee cups and suggests they go outside. He pulls the settle out into the sun on the edge of the porch and the two sit down.

"Dad hit 'cha last night?" Theron asks his uncle.

"Tried to. Not much to it, really—too drunk. Took a coupla swings at the air, but he was prob'ly swingin' at two a' me. I'm worried 'bout yer pa. He's never gonna 'mount ta much if'n he keeps swilling hooch th' way he does. It'll kill him if he doesn't kill someone else, first. I worry 'bout you and 'bout all th' animals. You can take care a yerself . . . have most a' yer life. Ain' the same wi' the girls and Luther. They need carin' for. Problem is, yer dad's more like one a' them. He needs carin' for, too. I seen 'im out tellin' his troubles t' Edna. Doubt she unnerstands much about whatever's troublin' 'im. She never had much to say when I been 'ere."

"Yeah. I seen 'im coupla times. He lies 'gainst her for warmth and tells her 'is troubles," adds Theron.

"Miss Emmons and I agree, you gotta go ta school in town and get yer high schoolin' done. World's changin', and ya can't go far without good learnin'. 'Sides, ya ain' had much parentin' since ya left the Clevelands. I spoke to Mrs. Morton, and you're gonna come board wi' me at her house while yer at school, and you can come 'ome here after school on Friday, but I want ya at the Morton's on Sunday night. Yer dad ain' gonna approve, but I'm goin' loco parentis on 'im, as we say in Latin class. I'm takin' over from 'ere." Adrian finishes, looking at his nephew. "If I have ta, I'll get Leonard to back me in managing yer schoolin'."

There's a long silence. Without looking up, Theron asks his uncle, "What about Dad? Who's gonna keep him outta trouble? Sometimes, he drinks so much 'e can't stand up, and forgets the chores. I worry 'bout him staggering around the barn with a lantern full a' kerosene. I worry 'bout 'im falling in the snow and freezing to death or fallin' through th' ice on Upper Pond when he's trappin'."

"I know ya do, but you can't take responsibility fer him *and* fer you. Ain' no way fer a young boy to grow. And, come ta think on it, for yer ma dyin' neither. In spite a' what yer dad keeps sayin', her death had nothin' to do with you."

"But it was me she was givin' birth to," Theron whispers, "like Dad says."

"Nonsense. Coulda been a brother or sister. Pure chance it was you. She'd a' died no matter what, less' someone was there t' help her. People die, and it's sad. You never knew 'er. Yer dad couldn't bear the guilt 'bout not bein' 'ere t' help 'er, and he tried ta pass it all ta you. Don' ya b'lieve it fer a minute. A' course he loves you, but he doesn't know how to love. Not sure he got much lovin' from our pa, neither. He drank some too. Ever'body did, so it seems."

"I wanna go to school. I like meetin' other kids. I like book learnin'. I jes' worry 'bout Dad here alone."

"I know, son, but the first thing ya learn in life is ya can't fix ever'one. Ya gotta fix yerself, and yer only half-baked. High school'll ready ya up for a good life. Weekends, we'll visit yer pa and help 'im with chores and see to the girls and Luther. Next summer, you can go back full-time if you want or ya can take a job in town. Mr. Morton always hires kids in the summer to work in his lumberyard."

Just then, Lionel steps through the door with two hands wrapped around a jar of coffee. He has a large blue welt below his left eye.

"Wha' you two plottin' 'gainst me?"

15

WHEN THERON'S NOT DOING ROUTINE OR SEA-
sonal chores, the summer brings him time
alone in the woods. On his ventures, Mags lopes along
behind and often disappears altogether in the ostrich
ferns and tufts of wet grass. Occasionally the cat will
freeze up at the rustle of a scurrying vole or the sudden
rise of a woodcock or partridge. Theron looks behind
to be sure Mags is nearby and, if not, calls for him
and waits.

Upper Pond and the basin are his two favorite
destinations within the several square miles he and
Mags range. He always brings his fishing pole, and
sometimes his .22, with an eye to creeling a few brookies or perch, or bagging the occasional rabbit or gray
squirrel for supper. In his creel Theron keeps a moss-
filled cotton sock, alive with night crawlers he stores
in a wood box near the chicken coop.

At Upper Pond, he picks his way carefully out to
the end of a fallen maple that stretches thirty feet out
into the water. He hangs onto protruding branches as
he picks his way along the slippery rotted wood out
to the end where the top of the trunk disappears into
the water. From here he can drop-fish in eight feet of

water and count on filling his creel with a dozen perch. Mags follows him out, but soon gets bored and returns to shore, where there are more of the distractions that interest him.

If they go to the basin, Theron can usually catch a few brookies, but the brookies are wilier; a half dozen is a good day's catch. He guts and dices one as a treat for Mags, while they sit together on a tuft of moss nearby. On hot days, he'll strip down and go for a dip in the basin or, if it's really hot, in Upper Pond, where he usually emerges with several leeches attached to his skin.

Theron relishes his time in the woods. The house and barn make him feel anxious. The ghosts of angry exchanges with his father over a chore not done or done wrong, or his father's drunken maunderings about the wrongs he's suffered, hang in the air there, but the woods are free of such concerns. He knows the paths, abandoned logging roads, waterways, and coverts that shelter deer and even an occasional black bear eating blackberries. Though he's heard tales from hunters and seen renderings in books of bobcat, lynx, and catamount, he has yet to see one in the Flats.

Lionel is both more and less a presence in Theron's life, and his drinking adds to Theron's responsibility to see that his father doesn't hurt himself. Farm chores can be dangerous and farm sustenance tenuous. While liquor's anodyne effect offers Lionel fleeting relief from loss, inadequacy, and guilt, the fugitive euphoria of Edna's borrowed intimacy dissipates in the cold ache of his hangovers. Theron has tried, on occasion, to talk with his father about why he drinks and why they never see anyone, but—like trying to imagine his mother—the effort to communicate with his father is futile.

One day he and Mags return from an afternoon gathering shang in and around the sugar works. The constant damp in the Flats supports a flourishing crop of wild ginseng, and the market for its fleshy root in various tonics sustains a vigorous trade. The sun is still high in the west, though the cool of evening's begun to set in. Mags bounds into the barn to inventory his thriving colony of mice, and Theron follows him, expecting to find his father milking, as the girls are in from the near pasture.

Luther the Belgian draft horse is lying on his side in the barnyard. Theron approaches him cautiously, but he immediately knows he's dead because of the gauzy look in his eyes. He hears an insistent lowing in the barn that tells him the girls have yet to be milked, but sees no sign of his father. Theron goes into the barn to find Lionel and ask him what happened to Luther. He hears his father's voice and goes quietly to the end of the stanchions where he once again finds Lionel curled up against Edna, his speech slurred. Theron listens and settles quietly on a stool behind Edna.

"I loss everthin' when she died. Never knowed no tenderness 'til she come along. 'S what I miss mos' ever' day, not havin' some tenderness, some'n ta 'old ya when you'se discouraged. Don' need much else in this life. I've al'ays been independent 'n' all. But no matters how 'ard ya work, a man still needs some tenderin' to survive. I know I ain't done right by Theron. 'E's a good boy 'n' lost 'is Ma, too. Poor boy lives alone wi' me. I ain' never been much of a father to 'im. He'd a' been better off stayin' wi' the Clevelands. I 'spect he'll be livin' wi' my brother nex' fall. Makes no never, no mind. I al'ays was by my lonesome anyways. Ain' nothin' gonna change none."

Theron, in tears, tiptoes out of the barn and up to the house, knowing he'll have to come back later to do the milking.

Theron builds up a small fire to take the chill off and notices how little wood is left. Pouring himself some milk, he eats the last piece of cornbread Miss Emmons sent over with Adrian. He reads his new book for an hour, but his father still hasn't come back to the house, so Theron goes down to milk, knowing the noise will disturb his father's reverie. He's surprised to find Edna upright, along with the other girls, and no sign of his father. Theron does the milking, forks hay down from the loft above, checks the water bowls, and then heads back to the house.

Lionel sits in his flannel undershirt in a straight-back kitchen chair instead of in his usual rocker; his barn coat and woolen shirt are on the floor next to the chair. He's slumped forward, clumsily nursing a mason jar in his left hand. Theron sees that Lionel's right arm is hanging limp and out of place. Below the elbow, the arm is bruised black and blue, and dried blood is flaking off.

"Dad, what happened to yer arm?" Theron shouts.

There's no answer, and Lionel looks away from his son. Surprised by his own anger, Theron shouts his question again, louder this time.

Lionel turns a sullen face toward his son and answers only, "Got hurt milkin'. Tryin' ta get Edna up off'n 'er pad an' she stepp'd on my arm, feels like it's broke."

"Yer lyin' agin, Pa. I 'as there watchin'. You was drunk, lyin' next ta Edna, tellin' 'er yer woes like ya do. You prob'ly fell t' sleep and she scrambled up and stepped on yer arm an' broke it.

"Look at cha. Yer a poor excuse for a man. I'm goin' ta the end of the road and get help. I don' wanna live like 'is no more. I ain' gonna be like you. Yer dyin'; this farm's dyin'. If'n it weren't fer Uncle Adrian and school, I'd be lyin' next ta ya. I'll be back wi' help. Stay by the fire."

16

T HE SIMPLE FRACTURE IN LIONEL'S ARM IS EASILY repaired, but the bruising turns septic and sclerosis in his liver weakens his remaining defenses. His latent affection for his son emerges, and Lionel begs Adrian to take him home to be with Theron, but his brother can't overrule Doc Jewett's insistence that Lionel remain in the hospital, explaining that if he goes home, he'll drink himself to death in a few days.

Lionel dies in his fifth week in the hospital and is removed by Jack Shank for a simple burial. Again Leonard Fogg, the county overseer, helps the family, finding funds for burial and a modest gravestone next to Thelma in Elmore Mountain Cemetery.

Theron's sense of loss is balanced by relief. Nine years of watching over his father, twenty-eight cows, an aging horse, a dwindling flock of hens, and a fire in a small woodstove ends. He knows he's lost his only parent and, when consoled, musters appropriate grief, but he's troubled that the grief hasn't come on its own.

Theron moves in with Adrian at the Mortons' place. Mags is allowed to board with them, and has even earned the affection of Mrs. Morton, who was doubtful at first. The cat sleeps curled up next to

Theron on his cot and accompanies him down to breakfast, where a bowl of warm milk awaits him.

Leonard and Adrian make arrangements for the farm. Neal Slater, the nearest neighbor, welcomes the opportunity to sell milk from more cows and to assume responsibility for the animals and fields. He adds the few remaining laying hens to his own stock. He agrees to a twelve-dollar-a-month lease for the farm with no set term. Ownership of the farm transfers to Adrian, and it's understood that he'll hold it in trust for Theron, who expresses an interest in farming it himself one day.

Theron thrives in high school. His time boarding at Mrs. Morton's with Adrian leaves him time after school to go to the public library, where he loves sitting at the large oak table to do his homework. If he finishes early and one of the oversize leather reading chairs is available, he curls up in it and reads, breathing in the luxuriant smell of saddle-soaped leather. He reads *The Adventures of Huckleberry Finn* and learns of life in the South along the Mississippi River, and he enjoys imagining himself in Huck's many adventures.

The library is warm, as are his breakfasts at Mrs. Morton's. After school, Theron and his uncle meet at the library and go on to share a meal at Peck's Diner downtown, where his favorite is the meatloaf special with gravy and mashed potatoes. Mrs. Peck always puts two rolls on the saucer, even though the "special" only calls for one.

Three meals, a warm bedroom, friends at school —including Ben—and a predictable cadence in his life restore Theron's belief that he can earn himself a future. Adrian reminds his nephew that he's never really had parents to speak of, and adds with a broad smile, "Yes, sir. Y'er yer own toad."

Theron begins noticing girls at school. No longer do they huddle by themselves, whispering as they used to in grade school; now they vie openly for the attention of the distracted boys, who usually feign disregard. Often, standing nervously in pairs, the girls groom themselves and one another and, on the rare occasion when they catch a boy's eye, smile and blush coquettishly. Theron sees all this and knows something has changed.

17

THERON'S YEARS AT PEOPLE'S GO QUICKLY. SUMMERS, he and Ben sign on with a camp boss logging in Woodbury, starting out as slash haulers and burners. Within a few months, as more newcomers sign on, each advances to limbing fells with a double-bitted axe or using a one-man saw. Enterprising workers are closely watched and highly valued, moving up the ranks from menial to skilled positions as limbers, sawyers, and buckers at one end of a two-man, six-foot crosscut saw, or "misery whip," as the old hands call it. Promising newcomers are paired up with experienced sawyers. Theron and Ben love the work. The boss, Eddie, takes note but shows no favor. Since hard work is expected, tacit approval is evidenced by advancing good workers up through the ranks so they learn the ropes. Eddie is also the scaler and grader and keeps track of stumpage for the landowner who's hired his crew.

Theron meets Lila Farnsworth in his senior year at People's. She transfers into his homeroom from Springfield High School near the end of the school year, two years after her father drowns in a log run on the Black River where it flows into the Connecticut

River. Lila's mother works in the Slack Shoddy Mill in Springfield as a sorter and carder. She can neither leave her job nor support her daughter, and so eventually sends Lila to live with her Aunt Grace in Hyde Park.

Lila has adjusted well to her new life in Hyde Park and Morristown. Even as a young girl in Springfield, she looked forward to visits from her Aunt Grace, whose visits later so visibly lifted her own mother's flagging spirits after her father's death in the Big River. In Lila's sophomore year, when she knew she would have to leave Springfield High to join her mother working in the mill to keep up the rent and groceries, Lila saw her prospects begin to unwind. Though she never complained, Anna Farnsworth could see the sadness in her daughter's eyes. Her beauty attracted the attention of older men in the mill, and Mrs. Farnsworth feared that her daughter's rising despair would lead her into a marriage and penury. It was then that she wrote to her sister Grace and asked if Lila might come and stay with her and her husband Clyde in order to resume her schooling.

Lila is a tall young woman, lithe and graceful. Her sorrel hair tumbles in two large ringlets onto her left shoulder. She has seen photographs of Evelyn Nesbit during the murder trial of her husband, and Lila decides that's who she wants to look like. When Lila enters a room, her beauty is noted. She's two years older than Theron and most of her classmates, which she explains by the two-year hiatus in her schooling when she went to work in the mill to make ends meet.

Theron is shy about approaching Lila and making himself known to her. She shows no interest in the social antics of her male classmates and keeps to herself. Annie Kitonis transferred in from Maine the same year as Lila. A Micmac, Annie keeps her own company and, in time, she and Lila become inseparable. Their close friendship frees them from needing to respond to overtures from their male classmates. Lila would like to be a nurse, but knows there will be no money from either her mother or aunt for nursing school. Annie wants to farm, and tells Lila she wouldn't be averse to doing so alone. She also tells her she's not drawn to the company of men.

Unaware of the belligerence brewing among aspiring empires in Eurasia, the members of the graduating class of 1907 are planning how they will eke out a living or whom they will marry. Several couples among Theron's classmates are already evident, and will soon lead to marriage by choice or by child. Girls who become pregnant by anonymous sires disappear into a distant home for unwed mothers, rarely returning to face the censure of friends and family. Such disappearances are commonplace. Pregnancies followed by marriage, however, are generally overlooked.

Theron is haunted by thoughts of Lila but is also shy. He doesn't approve of the way his male classmates behave with the women in their class. He doesn't see it for what it is, a courtship ritual to which many girls respond.

Lila has never questioned her attraction to Theron, however. It began in the classroom where she saw Theron's interest in his studies. Unlike many boys his age, he doesn't hide his curiosity. Whenever the teacher is facing the blackboard or immersed in correcting papers at her desk, a bloom of furtive glances, funny faces, and passed notes fills the unmonitored classroom. Theron ignores his companions' efforts to compete in the social hierarchy. Although he rarely volunteers or opens discussions, when called on he offers his answers, opinions, or questions about what he's reading or learning in history and science. Sometimes these elicit disdainful glances among his male peers.

Before moving to her aunt's, Lila had seen all she cared to of men, young and old, ruffling their male plumage in school and at the mill. She now knows she will only pay attention to serious young men. Theron is not competitive, and Lila likes this about him.

One afternoon when Theron is in the library, Lila comes in carrying a strap of books and her tin pencil box. She sits down at the oak table across from him, drops her books and pencils on the table, then looks up and smiles. Theron's nonplussed, and looks back at the book he's reading. Lila spreads out her papers, flattens the book she's studying, and begins writing in her tablet. Theron can't pay attention to what he's reading; he rereads the same paragraph in *Omoo* over and over again, wanting so much to look at Lila, but to do so would betray his interest and he'd be at a loss as to how to respond were she to acknowledge him.

The regulator wall clock above the librarian's desk chimes four o'clock, affording Theron an excuse to leave. He's due at Mrs. Morton's to help her plant her new rose bushes before he meets his uncle at Peck's for supper. Theron gathers his book under his arm, pushes back his chair noisily, and stands up.

Lila whispers, "See you at school tomorrow. Have a good night."

Theron turns and nods, saying only, "Yes, you, too," and leaves. He's embarrassed by his clumsiness.

Later that night, lying in his cot with his uncle Adrian snoring quietly next to him, Theron wishes he'd said something for which Lila might have remembered him. He wonders if he'll have a second chance.

18

LILA RETURNS TO THE LIBRARY AGAIN AND AGAIN.
Theron figures she, too, must prefer doing her
homework in the library instead of the after-school
study hall at People's. Lila nods and smiles at Theron
when she arrives. There are two long library tables,
and she always chooses the one at which Theron is
reading unless all the chairs are taken or he's sitting
in one of the leather chairs. But even then, she nods
and smiles.

Miss Ryder maintains silence in her library.
Whisperers, hummers, or chronic cougher-sneezers, as
she calls them, are banished after one warning. Habitual offenders' names are posted on the library's Tablet
of Shame, an upright clipboard on the librarian's desk.
Note passing is forgiven as long as it's not frequent.

One day late in the spring, Lila passes Theron a
note asking if he'd like to join her and Annie at a
sugar-on-snow party in Wolcott. Friends of Annie's
are boiling Saturday, and they invited her to bring a
friend to the sugar house. It's way out on East Hill
Road, not far from Wolcott Pond. Theron knows the
area well, having often hunted and fished it. In Wolcott Village, East Hill Road becomes East Elmore

Road, meandering south to Flats Road. Theron passes a note back saying he'd like to go, asking where and when to meet. A note comes back suggesting they go out to the front steps of the library, where they can talk above a whisper. Theron inhales deeply and nods his assent. He hasn't spoken to Lila before, only acknowledged her in nods and smiles—and now, a note.

Lila gathers her things and leaves. Theron pauses to look around and see if anyone has taken notice. He walks the long way out by the checkout desk and nods to Miss Ryder so he won't be seen leaving with Lila. They meet on the marble steps. Theron is unable to imagine himself as deserving of either her beauty or attention, and embarrassment and anxiety inhibit what little he manages to say. But Lila knows this, so she takes the initiative. They agree to meet Saturday morning in front of the grange in Wolcott. A horse-drawn buggy owned by Annie's friends will meet them there and drive them all up to the sugar works.

Theron says good-bye to Lila and walks into town, a half hour early to meet his uncle for supper. At Peck's he orders a coffee and sits in the booth replaying his conversation with Lila and the comfort and relief he heard in what little she said to him. He is encouraged by her calm and confident demeanor. How will he fare when they meet in Wolcott?

Saturday is sunny and about fifty degrees. Theron walks the six miles to Wolcott. He laughs at himself for being so early; the buggy won't meet them for another half hour. But Annie and Lila also arrive early, and Theron is relieved they're together. He finds it easier to talk with them both rather than just Lila.

It's hot inside the sugar house and most are outside in the sun. A young man is pouring sap into the evaporator at the arch end and a roaring fire of four-foot maple and oak logs blazes in the firebox below. Two men paddle boiling sap through the maze with square wooden spatulas. Another draws off a vial of thickening syrup at the spigot. He checks it for light, color, and viscosity and finally, as it cools, tastes it. He passes it to an older man. The older fellow purses up his lips, shakes his head sideways, and motions to pour it back in. A few minutes later, on the second try, the older man nods and the young man opens the spigot and fills a tinned bucket with amber syrup.

Annie yells to those outside that "syrup's up." Everyone steps back as her friend pours small patches of boiling syrup onto a pile of packed snow.

"Eat up!" she yells. "There's sour pickles, sap doughnuts, and black coffee inside. Don' overdo it, make yerself sick like the kids do every year."

Lila pulls a piece of taffying maple off the snow and approaches Theron with a smile. "Open wide, big fella. Yer gonna love this. Be sure an' eat a pickle now and then or the sweet'll get to ya."

Theron returns the favor and is surprised by an unexpected desire to kiss Lila, but he knows the shock it would produce and thinks it would end his chance to ever be her friend. So he is caught off guard when she kisses him gently on the cheek when no one's looking.

19

B Y GRADUATION, LILA AND THERON'S CLASSMATES
know them as a couple. Lila's beauty inspires occasional swains, but she offers them no encouragement. Theron is still haunted by fears and insecurities
but, with Lila's patience, he will learn they're his own.
He wants to enjoy her affection by understanding
what she sees in him, but that will take time, as he has
no way of seeing himself through her eyes. Lila is increasingly tender with him in public, but he's too shy
to reciprocate.

After graduation and consultation with his uncle,
Theron signs on again with his former camp boss in
Woodbury. The crew has relocated to Mackville, only
a few miles east of the farm as the crow flies, but
whatever roads might once have linked the two places
are now impassable. When the Flats was first logged,
a network of corduroy roads linked the logging camps.
But the cedar logs supporting horse-drawn sleighs,
rolling camp kitchens, and skidding teams have long
since rotted away into boggy deer runs. Few signs of
earlier enterprise survive in the second-growth woods.

Mrs. Morton explains to Adrian that her mother-
in-law is "going dotty" and will be moving in. At

Peck's, over a blue-plate special of baked beans, molasses, fatback, and bacon that ends with a generous side of Mrs. Peck's sour pickles, Adrian and his nephew decide they have little choice but to move back into the farmhouse. Neal will continue his leasehold, as neither Adrian nor Theron will have time to work the farm, but the farmhouse has been empty since Lionel died.

Adrian spends his summers tutoring and doing maintenance work on the school. Theron will be home only on weekends, as his crew works full daylight hours during the summers. He looks forward to living with his uncle, but is anxious about returning to his father's house, which he remembers as a place of anger and silence. He wants to keep seeing Lila, who has signed on as a bookkeeper at Morrill's Dry Goods, where she is also expected to work the counter in the fabric section, as needed.

The summers go quickly for Lila and Theron and they see more of each other. On his teacher's income, Adrian buys a sturdy used buggy to travel between the Flats and town. If Theron can't catch a ride from logging camp to Elmore, Adrian fetches him in the buggy. Lila still lives with her Aunt Grace, whose husband, Clyde, has a pony trap that Lila is free to use. The year Lila left Springfield to stay with them, her uncle sold his foundry business and retired, though he keeps a small forge at home. Grace and Clyde live in town, so

Grace manages her trading on foot and Lila can use the trap as she pleases.

Even after a few years, Theron still has anxieties about living in his father's house. He sometimes experiences an irrational fear that his father is about to appear. He wants more than anything to be with Lila, and often dreams of her after falling asleep on his lean-to shelf cot at camp. As is so often the case with dreams, Theron is never a character in his own dreams, some of which evoke a discomforting sexual response in him.

He's never yet had Lila to the house, although she has asked about it many times. So one Sunday, Theron asks Adrian to leave word at Morrill's that she's invited over for a picnic.

Adrian sees his nephew's reticence, but also his affection for Lila. Although he never married, Adrian is no stranger to women and encourages his nephew to welcome Lila's affections. He asks what makes him nervous about seeing Lila, and Theron tells him he's worried about what he will say to her and how it will sound.

That Sunday Theron is picking carrots, small turnips, and radishes he and Adrian planted to augment their store-bought supplies when he hears Lila's trap coming down the road and feels at once a thrill and the anxiety that haunts him. She pulls into the yard, wraps the reins around a fence rail, pats the brindle pony on his shoulder, and walks over to Theron, smiling. Mags lolls on the porch settee in the sun.

"How you doin' there, logger? I don't see no cuts or bruises."

Theron returns her smile, and his anxiety ebbs. She takes him by the hand and they walk onto the porch. She stops to pet Mags, who looks up with gratitude. He's now quite old, and more somnolent than he was when he was first invited in from the barn.

"I brought some things for our picnic. You're not gonna make me eat turnips, are ya?"

"No," Theron says with a chuckle. "Adrian made some pork sandwiches, and we have pickles. What'd you bring?"

"Be a surprise, I think you'll like it. Wish I'd had some of them fresh carrots yer pullin' up when I was bakin'."

"I got a jar of cider from Neal down the road, as well. Any idea where you'd like to go this afternoon?"

"You live here, take me where you want. I'm not much on climbin', though."

Lila and Theron go in the kitchen to finish packing the picnic hamper Lila's brought. Theron apologizes for the unlived-in appearance of his father's house. Adrian is nowhere in sight.

The two head off about noon. Mags follows for a bit, and eventually gives up and heads back to the house. Theron suggests they go to the glen and maybe try to catch a few brookies. In a clearing nearby is a large stand of lady's slipper and jack-in-the-pulpit that he's visited every year since he discovered the glen. He's never had anyone except Mags to show it to until this day.

Theron and Lila sit on a damp, moss-covered outcrop with their bare feet in the water. Theron is relieved to find his anxieties occur more in her absence than in her company now. She knows to fill silences that might cause him embarrassment, and recounts to him her upbringing in Springfield. When he asks about her father, he sees her discomfort. This confirms his sense of ineptitude and, through her tears, she can't fix this. He apologizes even as she assures him it's not his fault. She pauses and sniffles, saying only that she still misses her father. She goes on to recall how hard her father and mother worked to sustain even the modest second-story apartment they lived in on the outskirts of Springfield.

Lila recovers, dries her eyes with Theron's flannel shirt sleeve, and launches into a description of the spring log drives her father worked when the driving dams upriver were opened to create a massive freshet propelling the logs, destined for the big mill in Bellows Falls, into the main river at Hoyt's Landing. But when a log boom upstream between Wells River and Woodsville, New Hampshire, broke open and released four thousand cords of pulp, all hell broke loose in the lower river and a half dozen men, including Lila's father, drowned trying to break up jams at various points in the river.

Theron is enthralled. He has been learning the full range of logging operations in the woods, but has only heard old loggers talk about the river drives that Lila's description brings to life. He talks about his experience on a two-man saw and recounts an incident in which he and a newcomer were manning a six-footer. The spotter was distracted and missed the initial sway of the sixty-foot white oak they were cutting. Theron heard the trunk crack, looked up, and saw the tree falling against the back cut and pinching the saw. He yelled at the other sawyer to move, but his partner's focus was fixed on the falling trunk. When it landed and the hinge snapped in the cut, the pinched saw sprang into the air and caught his partner in the forearm. He lost a lot of blood from his badly mangled forearm, but Doc Jewett saved the arm and the boy returned to work the following winter.

Lila fishes around in the basket, withdraws their sandwiches and pickles, and lays the spread out on a hand towel. Theron dangles a worm below the bank on the far side of the stream.

"Let's eat," Lila suggests. Theron lays his pole down on the·moss. To his surprise, Lila leans over and kisses him on cheek. To Lila's surprise—and Theron's—he reciprocates, gently kissing her on the lips.

She throws her arms around him. He pauses for a second, and without thinking whispers a question to her, "Would ya ever consider marryin' me?"

She draws back in surprise and with a broad smile says, "I'se afraid *I'd* have to do the proposin'! Yes, I'd happily be your wife."

Theron sees the tip of his rod dip into the water and grabs it in time to sink his hook into an eight-inch brookie.

20

THE WEDDING IS PLANNED FOR THE FOLLOWING May. Theron and Lila do their best to put aside a little money and take every opportunity to see one another. Hearing the news, Adrian notifies Neal that Theron and Lila will be taking over farming in the spring.

On the weekends Lila works at Morrill's, and Theron and Adrian fix up the house, undoing years of Lionel's neglect. The house is well built, with a solid, dry-laid stone foundation, oak sills, and balloon framing, but the exterior and interior finishes are chipped and peeling. The windows need to be reputtied, and the four weather-side windowsills have dry rot and need replacing. The kitchen linoleum is worn through, so they tear it up, block sand, and reshellac the pumpkin pine floorboards. The stove needs new asbestos seals, a piece of broken mica replaced in the front fire door, and reblacking; aside from some blistering chrome on the warming-shelf trim, the Glenwood looks like new when they finish. Adrian replaces the gasket seals in the sink valve to stop the endless dripping, which proves a mistake the following winter when the pipes freeze up for the first time in memory.

Adrian occasionally stops by to see Mrs. Morton, to catch her up on the news and share a pot of coffee. On one visit she loads his buggy with some old blankets, bed linens, extra flatware, and a cast-iron Dutch oven that needs sanding and reseasoning. Mr. Morton contributes some tools he no longer uses: a post-hole digger, an iron pry bar, a peavey, a double-sided axe, wooden block and tackle, and a rusty chicken waterer, all in usable condition. Adrian delivers the treasures to Theron, who's thrilled with the haul and touched by their generosity.

That night the two settle in to share a chicken that Theron has been simmering all day in salt, cider, and a handful of green onions. It falls apart when he ladles it into their ironstone bowls; they abandon their forks, eating the carcass with their fingers and slurping the broth directly from the bowls.

"You ready for married life, boy? Y' haven't had much learning 'bout wimmin 'n' all."

"I 'spect I'll figure it out on my own. Don' need your learnin' on the matter. 'Sides, where'd ya get all yer learnin' on 'em? Y' ain' never been married I know of."

"I s'pose Lila'll teach ya what ya need ta know ta please 'er."

"None yer beeswax what we do in our time. Tend ta yer own business."

"Jes' tryin' a be a good uncle 'n' all. I'se here if'n ya need me."

"I don', but thanks fer askin'," Theron answers with finality.

"Did ya hear the one about the two bulls on the hilltop?" Adrian persists.

"No, do I wanna?"

"The young bull says ta the old bull, 'Let's run down and fuck a cow.' The old bull looks at the young bull and says, 'No, let's walk down and fuck 'em *all*. There's a lesson in there."

"Not sure I unnerstand the lesson." Theron smiles in spite of himself.

"It's a message 'bout takin' life slow and doin' more in it."

"I'll think on it. Still not sure I get it."

"Ya never had no ma, safe ta say. B'lieve it or not, menfolk learn more from their mas than they do from their pas. Pas teach 'bout how ta do things; mas 'bout how ta git 'long in life. Ya got a lotta learnin' ahead a' you with Lila. Gotta be careful not to try and get motherin' from a wife. Ya'll lose her if ya do. Bein' a wife ain' bein' a mother. They'se different, ya see.

"Yer own pa never recovered from Thelma's dying. He blamed you, which 'as all wrong and don' ya ever forget it. Wasn't yer fault, you was jes' bein' born's all. We all wan' tenderness. We hate sayin' it's so, but it's true fer all of us. Me, too. It's the greatest gift . . . someone to tender ya, hold ya, and make ya feel loved 'n' all. You remember that when ya marry Lila. She'll be wantin' tenderness too.

"Only place my brother ever got tenderin' was from a dumb cow, an' only then when he 'as too drunk ta know the difference between a cow and a woman. Sad ta see." Adrian shakes his head.

Theron sits quietly, staring at his plate and sorting through his chicken and his uncle's advice. Adrian gets up and carries the two plates to the sink. He scrapes the remains from the two plates into the biddy pail by the sink where food scraps pile up for the hens, to be augmented by their daily handfuls of cracked corn.

"Goin' ta bed. You should too; you'll need yer rest. Tomorrow's Sunday, and Lila'll be out. Don' forget what I'm tellin' ya. You pay attention to that woman. I ain' seen better yet. You treat 'er right and she'll do the same ta you. Lovely girl."

With that Adrian retires to his dead brother's ground-floor room, curls up under the quilt, and falls asleep. Theron tosses a log on the fire and goes up to his room to read *Robinson Crusoe*.

21

SUNDAY IS ABLAZE IN SUNLIGHT. LILA ARRIVES EARLY in her pony cart with a basket of dinner items for the three of them, but to Theron's surprise, he finds a note in the kitchen from Adrian saying he's gone to town for Sunday dinner with the Mortons and asking Theron to give his best to Lila.

Theron and Lila sit on the front porch until noon, facing into the sun and talking about the wedding and who'll be invited and who'll come—just their family and friends. Though neither of them are churchgoers, they agree they'll have it at the Methodist Society Church in Elmore, as there'll be less fuss there. They share a pot of coffee sweetened with maple syrup and dappled with floating drops of butterfat from the rich cream. As Lila unpacks their dinner, Theron suggests they go back out into the sun and eat on the porch. The two of them carry the kitchen table out along with two chairs. Lila brings out a platter of sliced ham and some potato salad made with sour pickles, green onions, and hard-boiled eggs. The two eat side by side on the narrow porch, facing out, all the while talking of the farm work they're planning and what extra Lila might do to add to their milk check income. Working at Morrill's in the fabric department when she isn't keeping books, she's become adept at needlework, and her favorite customers take the time to show her new patterns and stitches.

After lunch they bring in the dishes, wash up, and cover the food left on the platter with a clean dishcloth. Theron suggests they hike up to the pond and see what waterfowl they might find. Loons, wood ducks, and mallards are all frequent visitors, and on occasion he has seen a great blue heron drop in to fish for a pumpkinseed or brown trout.

Theron's favorite spot is an expanse of tufted ground moss near the fallen tree from which he fishes. Lila spreads out on an afghan Theron has brought. With a pat of her hand, she motions to Theron to join her. As he sits down he feels a wave of embarrassment, almost as if they're sharing a bed for the first time. Lila senses his discomfort, and takes his hand.

Theron fears that something is expected of him, and he doesn't know what, like the first time he kissed Lila. He knows he must never impose himself on her, though he can't imagine how that would happen. He's afraid only that he'll do something that will cause her to leave him. Lila senses his fear and asks nothing of him. They lie there quietly in the sun. Theron begins to feel more comfortable and kisses her. She turns to him, smiling and rewards his courage with a warm embrace.

The two pick up their conversation about their life together: how many children they might have, and their hopes for the farm. Lila spots a family of wood ducks on the far side of the pond near the shore.

As the sun dips and a fog forms over the water, Lila says she must set out for home in the trap before it gets dark. Theron rolls up the afghan and drapes it over his shoulder. Lila approaches him and gives him a standing hug. Theron feels the full length of her woman's body against his own and is relieved of his fear. He knows he's loved by the woman standing in front of him, even though he doesn't know why. Lila understands it's the first time he's ever known love or the warmth of a woman's embrace.

As they walk down through the maidenhair ferns back toward the farm, they hear the two-tone cry of a loon from back on the pond. And soon the call is answered by another.

22

THERON AND LILA HAVE BEEN MARRIED FOR FIVE years. Over the kitchen table is a framed and yellowing copy of *The News and Citizen* report of their wedding:

Saturday, May 11, 1912: The wedding of Theron Wright of Hardwood Flats and Lila Farnsworth was held this Saturday in the Elmore Methodist Society Church. Miss Farnsworth hails from Springfield and, more recently, from Hyde Park. The service was performed by the Reverend Lester Calhoun and was well attended by local family and friends. Her mother Mrs. Anna Farnsworth was prevented from joining the festivities due to ill health, being unable to make the arduous journey by train and jitney from Springfield.

Guests included Grace and Clyde Collette, the bride's aunt and uncle; Adrian Wright, the groom's uncle and a teacher of English and world history at the People's Academy; Linwood, Emma, Ben, Becky, and Linda Cleveland, the groom's foster family; Leonard Fogg, the county overseer; Wanda

Demars, a family friend who helped care for the groom as a child after his mother's untimely death; Doc Jewett and his nurse, Elise Jackson, who oversaw the birth of the groom in 1888; Neal Slater, the groom's nearest neighbor in Hardwood Flats; Clara Emmons, the groom's Elmore grade school teacher; Miss Ryder, the town librarian; Mr. and Mrs. Jack Morton, Wright family friends; and Mr. Boright and Mrs. Fletcher, the groom's English teachers from People's Academy.

The newlyweds will make their home at the farm in the Flats formerly owned by the groom's father, Lionel Wright, who went to his maker in 1904. A light meal of egg salad and ham salad sandwiches, lemonade, and a two-tiered wedding cake followed the service at the town grange, where fun was had by all.

—WINONA LAMBERT, Elmore correspondent to the *News and Citizen*

Lila keeps her bookkeeping job at Morrill's Dry Goods to supplement their monthly creamery check. But winter travel via the trap and pony her aunt and uncle gave them as a wedding present is difficult except on the fairest days. Ida Morrill assigns another girl to the fabrics and notions department and lets Lila continue with the bookkeeping, as that lends itself more easily to her periodic absences.

Theron reinvests every spare dollar of their income acquiring new heifers at the weekly commission sales in Cady's Falls and also buys a retired bull for a dollar to freshen the girls and maintain their lactations. He's up to twenty-two cows and has doubled his milk check.

Lila returns home one night, breathless with news from Uncle Adrian. He's been called up in the new draft and will be sent overseas to fight the Germans. Theron and Lila know only what they read in newspapers, often a month or two in arrears, that Lila brings home from Mrs. Morrill. Theron doesn't fully understand the import of his uncle's news. He knows soldiers have been called up before, but the term *conscription* is as new to him as it is to much of the rest of the country. He and Lila read of the war brewing in Europe and remember discussing with surprise the German sinking of the British passenger ship *Lusitania* two years back.

Adrian comes out to visit the following weekend. Over Sunday breakfast he expresses greater fear of losing his teaching job at People's than of donning a uniform and sailing overseas to fight. The news troubles Lila and Theron, however, and has them combing old newspapers to better understand the scale of violence and danger Adrian is about to encounter.

Adrian must report to Boston for duty in mid-June. Theron, Lila, and his best friend and teaching colleague, Bruno, see him off at the train station in Morristown, waving and forcing smiles.

Adrian returns home in seventeen months, a changed man, missing half an arm and bearing the new name his comrades have given him, Stub. He doesn't want to impose on Theron and Louise, so he asks Mrs. Morton if he might again board there, as her mother died of pneumonia while he was overseas. Mrs. Morton is pleased to have Adrian in her home again.

Adrian's position at People's had been filled by a young woman, with the understanding that she'd be reassigned when Adrian returned from the front. But Adrian comes home in late March, and the school year has only two months to go. It's decided that Miss Palmer will teach out the year and Adrian will start again in the fall of 1919. He resumes his former summer work, working alone to maintain the school buildings and grounds over the summer break, and boarding with the Mortons.

The loss of an arm doesn't disqualify a good teacher, but loss of scholarly mettle does. Adrian's first few weeks back in the classroom are marked by unexplained absences, occasional breakdowns, and shouted rants at people not in the classroom. He begins each world history class reading to his fearful and confused students with passages from the war poetry of Wilfred Owen and Siegfried Sassoon.

Concerned with what he is hearing from students, parents, and occasionally from Adrian's classroom, the new principal, Mr. Connors, sits in to observe one of Adrian's classes and determines that one of their best teachers is no longer "of sound mind." Adrian is dismissed without pay. His colleagues don't recognize the person they knew, nor can they understand what's brought about this change in their friend. But they cannot imagine and have yet to read of the horrors he went through in France.

Mrs. Morton has heard the gossip and knows the whys and wherefores of Adrian's dismissal but, like many in town, is also aware of his service to his country and knows him to be a kind and thoughtful person. Mr. Morton, however, expresses concern to his wife that Adrian has been holed up in his room since leaving his job at People's and is seen only for breakfast coffee and sometimes at lunch. Adrian no longer converses with them, but instead brings a book to the breakfast nook and reads while the Mortons chat uncomfortably with one another.

"I don't know what happened over there, but he isn't himself," Mrs. Morton tells her husband one day when they're alone. Mrs. Morton is a light sleeper and often hears Adrian pacing in his room down the hall, reciting something she can't quite make out. She'll hear him go quiet for a time and then begin sobbing. Mr. Morton sleeps through it, but wakes up one night when he hears Adrian bound down the stairs, slam the front door, and begin ranting at someone on the front lawn. He gets up to calm him and, as he steps out on the lawn in his bathrobe, sees lights go on in the neighbors' houses.

The next night, alone at dinner, Mr. and Mrs. Morton agree they can't continue to offer Adrian room and board. The next day, Doc Jewett comes by the hardware store to have a pane of glass cut and Mr. Graves asks him what he's heard about Adrian. Doc conveys what he's heard by way of rumor and what he's heard from medical colleagues in White River Junction and Albany about boys coming home changed from the war, suffering from severe mental disturbances. Doc offers to see Adrian, and Mr. Graves agrees to pass the offer on to him.

When Mr. Graves arrives home after work, he learns from his wife that Adrian has packed up his few things and gone. Word of Adrian's departure reaches Theron and Lila when Neal stops by on his way back from delivering milk to the creamery, where he heard the news. Both Lila and Theron are surprised that Adrian left no word of where he was going or for how long. It will be thirteen years before they hear anything of their uncle again.

Their sense of loss from Adrian's sudden departure from town is compounded by the disappearance of Mags, on whom Theron has lavished so much attention over the years. Mags, now decrepit, doesn't appear for his evening snack. This has never happened, and Theron expects the worst. He tells Lila he's going to look for him in the barn and returns a half hour later. He's heard that when a cat knows its life is ending, it simply goes off into the woods and waits patiently for death to come.

They live for a while with no house cat until, one day after milking, Theron hears the sound he heard when he was seven years old while watching milk snakes. He moves the tin-lined grain box to find a mother cat in the corner, on some hay, nursing five kittens. Several weeks later, when the kittens' eyes are open and they're venturing farther from their mother, Theron takes Lila by the hand and walks her down to the milk house to choose their next house cat. She cuddles them all, handing them off one by one to Theron to review, and finally chooses another wide-toed tiger they name Mags. Lila likes to imagine that the earlier Mags sired this new litter, the rest of which will inhabit the barn.

23

LILA THINKS OFTEN OF HER FATHER—NOT ABOUT HIS
death in the Big River, but about how much she
wishes he was still alive, because she has questions
about how men are and what they want. Unlike her
father, her husband is quiet, and she senses he's holding in a question he doesn't know how to ask. She
knows, too, that Theron spent his childhood parent-
ing an alcoholic father, whereas Heb Farnsworth
was always demonstrative in his affection for his
wife and daughter, teasing out their secret joys and
sadness and offering good-hearted advice on life's per-
plexities. Lila has no doubts about her choice of
Theron as a husband, or her love for him—or his for
her—but she knows it will fall to her to answer a question he hasn't asked.

In spite of their shared affection, Lila's patient
tenderness, and Theron's easy surrender to her intima-
cies, no children come their way. Theron and Lila have
always imagined sharing their farm with children; the
hardscrabble nature of dairy farming encourages large
families. Even so, Lila and Theron continue to thrive
on each other's company and subsist on their thirty-
four acres, making do with what they produce to con-

sume, trade, or sell. Their twelve cleared acres are fenced along with another six acres of rough pasture. Their twenty-two cows graze the land, producing about twenty-two hundred pounds of milk a week. The creamery pays $2.08 per hundred pounds of weight, so Theron brings in about forty-five dollars weekly for his milk. Their other sixteen acres are second-growth timber, and each year Theron manages to clear another acre or two to transplant the wild apple trees he finds in the Flats. From rootstock given to him by their neighbor Neal, he starts rhubarb and asparagus patches that he top-dresses with old manure. Lila and Theron periodically look in on Neal, who is now in his early seventies.

Lila has kept up her friendship with Annie, though it's not been easy, as Annie's small farm is several miles away on Elmore Mountain Road. Annie raises potatoes and asparagus, keeps sheep for wool, and sells spring lambs to urbanites buying up nearby farms as the bank auctions empty them of their goods and families. Annie has a quarter horse, Buster, and enjoys barrel racing, although there are few women with whom to compete. In her meadow she has a figure-eight riding arena with painted barrels set up and practices in her spare time while Beth looks on and times her with a pocket watch.

Annie and Beth met at the town grange after graduation. Beth was looking for a position as a hired hand. Annie could ill afford an employee, but offered Beth a job working with her for a share of the harvest. They've been together ever since, in a time when no assumptions are made about women choosing to live and work together; it is understood that exigency throws many people together to survive.

Annie's neighbors revel in the thick, pale-green asparagus spears she sells in bunches in late spring and buy fifty-pound burlap sacks of potatoes from her in late summer. Though she sells a few "hangers," most of her spring lambs end up in the walk-in cooler at Patch's Market in Morristown, where they're cut up and sold by the chop, rack, or shoulder to locals. At Lila's urging, Annie and Beth also plant and sell cut flowers to their increasingly upscale neighbors who can afford such frills. Lila knows women can talk more freely about matters of the heart, and her occasional discussions with Annie over shared chores sustain her and complement her affection for Theron.

At times Annie will ride Buster over to Lila and Theron's, unannounced, with the excuse of helping Lila out with a seasonal chore, usually setting out her countless flats of spring vegetable starts or helping her with the fall canning. During these visits they recall past excitements and disappointments or share their anxieties about weather, tool breakdowns, reports of neighbors in distress, or the occasional snippets of dated national and international news they hear. Just as often, however, they work in silence, focused on the task at hand and content in one another's company. After the chores they sit on the veranda with a pitcher of ice tea—or cider, if any's left—and chat quietly about news of former teachers, classmates, town eccentrics, epic misbehaviors: the petty tragedies and delights of community.

On one of her visits Annie brings Lila a dog-eared copy of James Fenimore Cooper's *The Last of the Mohicans*. Its calf-hide cover is brittle, and a pale blue ribbon holds the book's loose pages in sequence, as many of them have broken free of the hand-sewn binding. The pages themselves are rife with rust-colored foxing, but the book's elegant typography still radiates.

Annie finds an entire set of Cooper's *Leather-stocking Tales* at a library sale and buys them for a dollar, never expecting to read them. But after reading *The Last of the Mohicans* and passing it on to Lila, she is drawn into the stories of danger and derring-do and passes the books on to Lila on successive visits as she finishes them.

Lila loves the fragile books and enjoys reading them. On nights when Theron doesn't fall easily into sleep, she reads aloud to him until she hears him snoring softly next to her. The fraught tale of Alice and Cora's escort to Fort William Henry comes alive, and Lila imagines herself in the narrative.

The oil lamp on the bedstead provides just enough light for one person to read and, even then, its sulfurous glow confirms Lila's perception that her eyes are losing their youthful acuity. She cleans the oil lamp's glass globe each morning and sets it on Theron's side of the bed in case he wants to read, but most nights he is too tired and lies quietly on his back until he rolls over on his side facing her and falls asleep.

24

IN 1932 LILA AND THERON RECEIVE A SCRAWLED POST-card from Adrian. He's living in a "Hooverville" in the District of Columbia with fifteen thousand other World War I veterans and their families, and they have formed a brigade called the Bonus Army. They're trying to redeem veterans' cash benefit certificates received a decade earlier. Adrian adds that he hopes to find work in the new Civilian Conservation Corps in Connecticut; he declares himself "alive and well enough," and the card is signed "Uncle Stub."

Later that year a letter arrives from an anonymous friend of Adrian's, informing them, "Your Uncle Stub died riding the rails trying to get back home after armed forces sent in by General MacArthur drove all the veterans out of their encampment."

In 1933 Theron buys a pair of Percherons at a farm auction in Woodbury. Such auctions are now becoming more common as the financial noose tightens around more tenuous farms during the Great Depression. Farmers who borrow to extend their holdings or who mechanize too soon often fall victim to repossessions—or worse, these auctions in which they must part with everything. Theron and Lila are content, however, to live without debt and buy what they need with cash.

By the time the nation begins to recover from the Depression, in 1934, Theron has acquired at auctions a side-bar cutter, a side rake, a tedder, a haylift, and two hay wagons. These auctions were not a form of entertainment to Theron, as they could be for many; he constantly fretted about acquiring the chattels of those he saw watching from the sidelines as their possessions were sold off to the highest bidder. Yet he also knew that each purchase he made would help offset a family's indebtedness. Sometimes he saw himself and Lila in their faces, and this made him uncomfortable; he would always settle up and leave as quickly as he could after he'd bought what he came for—at or for less than the price he was willing to pay.

During haying, Theron needs Lila to ride on the hay wagon and pitch hay to the rear as the haylift fills the front. When the wagon's full and Lila is high atop the pile of loose hay, they drive into the hayloft in the upper barn and unload with the trolley and hayfork that Theron and Neal installed. With no way to know the weather, they usually get two cuts each summer with the horses Sadie and Norma pulling first the side-bar cutter, the tedder, and the side rake and, finally, the haylift and the wagon.

Covered with chaff, they return to the kitchen before milking and dusk, and Lila pours them both a tall glass of her crabapple cider or her homemade tomato juice. Theron then puts Sadie and Norma away, hangs their working tack on the outer wall of Norma's box stall, and begins milking while Lila makes supper.

Theron spends a lot of time "harvesting stone," as he delights in telling Lila, and teases her about finding a recipe for stone soup. Just when he thinks he's finally cleared a garden plot of stones and boulders, the coulter on his plow bumps over another. Each spring, frost heaves up new stones from the damp earth. Sadie and Norma know to stop while Theron takes out his crowbars and levers it up out of the furrow. Ones smaller than a turkey he lugs over and adds to the rubble wall, which grows higher each year. If a rock is "only the tit of an iceberg," as he says, he fetches a shovel, digs at its perimeter until he can get a chain around it, and then unhooks the plow and hitches Sadie's tugs to the chain, urging her on while he works the stone from behind with a bar until it frees up and somersaults up onto the meadow. He then unhitches the ropes from the tugs, and he and Sadie walk back to the shed to get the stoneboat he made with a header of cast iron, a length of old log chain, and some hornbeam planks. He levers the boulder onto the stoneboat and Sadie hauls it to the edge of the field.

Lila's industry comes to fruition in the garden plots Theron clears for her, and in her kitchen, adding considerably to their income. She cans fruit, tomatoes, and venison; pickles eggs, garlic, and cucumbers in vinegar; and makes jams and jellies from wild blackberries and blueberries, cultivated red currants, and raspberries. She sells the excess butter she churns, rolling it into balls wrapped in cheesecloth. The shang she and Theron harvest farther out in the Flats she dices and preserves in honey, then sells the five or six pint jars she produces for three dollars apiece at the fall fair. For the last few years, one woman has bought all her jars of ginseng, and the proceeds pay the property tax on their farm.

Lila derives great satisfaction from raising her fruits and vegetables and tending her random garden plots. She understands that the pleasure she derives from her gardens offsets the sadness she feels at their not being able to have children. She knows, too, that for some women children are poor compensation for their joyless marriages. But her marriage is strong, so the sadness of its infertility is balanced by the fecundity of her many gardens.

The garden brings Lila pleasure throughout the year. The seeds she starts in February and March are set out in April and May into cold frames Theron made for her out of old windows, and then finally into the garden beds she has prepared for their arrival. Summers she spends culling weeds and thinning overcrowded plants, and the far-ranging biddies keep down bugs, insects, and crawlers. In August the major harvest begins, lasting into the following February, when she pulls chard and kale from the deep snow in the bed near the barn. The fall and winter months bring canning, drying, fermenting, and root cellaring.

The pleasure of working side by side with Theron during haying and sap runs is enough, as their exertions preclude any idle talk other than what's needed to work together. Theron's not a talker, but Lila now thinks she knows the question that's been in him for all their years together: he can't fathom why Lila chose to be with him and why she responded with joy to his proposal. She imagines that, never having experienced the love of either parent, he has no way of understanding what there is in him to love. It's a question Theron cannot ask, and Lila cannot answer in words; she knows instead it falls to her to answer it with her attentions. Theron, too, shows his love for Lila in small ways. She often finds a bouquet of wildflowers in a mason jar on their bedstead or a moistened newspaper on the veranda wrapping a bunch of bare-root lady's slipper, jack-in-the-pulpit, or white trillium carefully dug up and ready for her to transplant into one of her gardens.

After chores and supper, the two are happy but tired, so they turn in. It's always been their habit to retire together in the evening, regardless of chores done or undone; it's their favorite time together. Lila pretends to look Theron over for small cuts and bruises, bug bites, or rashes, and sometimes applies a soothing balm if she finds anything. It's mostly a pretext, though, to give her the opportunity to let him know how much he is loved, and occasionally for more. When she's done, Theron takes her in his arms and holds her gently to him until she's breathing quietly in her sleep, then soon after he, too, drifts off. Later she might disengage momentarily to arrange herself more comfortably in their bed, but only after he's snoring quietly.

Theron finds little time to read, but he knows Lila's eyesight is waning. In the evening, if they retire early, Lila will sometimes prevail on Theron to read to her, if only for a half hour. Hearing Theron read aloud brings her pleasure, and she knows he loves to read and would do so more often if he did not work as hard as he does.

In the spring of 1939, Lila and Theron get word that their neighbor Neal Slater has died. Elise Jackson has been replaced as home-care nurse by Rena LeClaire, who can be cranky when crossed, but she takes good care of the many elderly folk living alone. For a while now she has dropped in to see Neal every two weeks or so and brought him news, his mail, and some extra groceries. But one day she finds him sitting motionless in his rocker by the woodstove, wrapped in his quilt. His head is tilted to the side and his eyes are open. She knows this look. After checking for a pulse, she uses Neal's phone to call the undertaker.

Several weeks later, Willard Sanders calls on Theron and Lila to let them know that Neal has left them the John Deere model D tractor he bought a number of years back, his brand new Evinrude chainsaw, and another fourteen acres of meadow abutting their own. The house, barn, and remaining twenty-two acres will go on the market and the proceeds will go to Neal's nephew, a trapper who lives in Barton.

Lila and Theron are astonished at Neal's bequest; the John Deere is the first powered vehicle they've owned. The model D has a drawbar on the back and a bucket loader on the front. Its 38-horse engine is started by hand-spinning a fly-wheel capstan that, once running, can belt-drive a cordwood saw. All their old equipment is horse-drawn, but it can still be made to work with Neal's tractor. Theron has only to weld on new hitch hardware to attach to the drawbar. The additional acreage will mean more hay, something they've needed a few times when long winters drag on into late springs.

At supper that evening they discuss what will become of Norma and Sadie, and decide to keep them for a year until they're sure their first tractor's a reliable replacement for the team, in part because they know that buying both grain and fuel will be too expensive in the long run.

25

ONE SUNDAY JUST AFTER DINNER, LILA AND THERON hear a car coming up the driveway and go out onto the veranda to see who it is. The doors open on a Ford Model A, and Aunt Grace and Uncle Clyde emerge. Lila lets out a whoop and runs to embrace her aunt, whom she rarely has occasion to see, but she can tell immediately from her embrace and moist face that she is the bearer of bad news.

"What's wrong, Aunt Grace? Is it Ma?"

Aunt Grace breaks down, and Clyde steps up to her and holds her by the waist.

"Your mother died two days ago, and we just got word last night. It was late, or I'd have come right over; there wasn't anything we could've done in the middle of the night. I thought maybe you'd wanna come with Clyde and me down to the funeral in Springfield. It's a long drive, but we can get there in a day and stay with Mattie Nutting, who called to let me know. She's already made the funeral arrangements, and your ma will be buried on Tuesday. I knew you'd wanna be there. I was hopin' you'd come back with us to Hyde Park today, so we can get an early start. If we set out tomorrow morning, we should be there by sundown."

Lila looks at Theron, who puts his arm around her and draws her to him. "I'm so sorry, hon. Ya gotta go. I'll see ta things here. Ya need to be with yer family, times like this. Go on, get yer things together."

Mags begins rubbing his back against Theron's ankle and Theron bends down and scoops up the rangy tiger by his belly, cradles him in his other arm and scratches him between the ears. Lila hears the purring and forces a wet smile as she realizes again her husband's gentleness, then goes into the house to pack an overnight bag.

On the way back to Hyde Park, Lila learns that her mother finally succumbed to the rheumatoid arthritis that plagued her older years and kept her from her daughter's wedding.

"Mattie told us Doc Harris said 'er spinal cord just wore out . . . said it was collapsing and pinching nerves that kep 'er alive. Said it could only 'a been a relief from the pain she was feeling near the end."

Lila is grateful she's riding in the back seat and can give vent to her sadness and tears. She is not by nature an overly emotional person, believing such displays a sign of weakness or wile. She tells herself she abandoned her mother, knowing how sick she was and how sick she was to become. She was in a wheelchair even when Lila and Theron were married and, for the first time, Lila questions her choices.

Grace kept up occasional correspondence with Mattie, as Anna could read but wrote only under duress, recalling the grade school humiliations of her misspellings at the blackboard. Mattie had told Grace in one of her letters that Dr. Harris had prescribed laudanum, which relieved much of her pain and enabled her to sleep.

Lila falls asleep thinking of her mother and how she wishes she had been with her when the end came.

"We're here," Clyde says as the car stops. They've arrived at a modest yellow painted Victorian on the main street of Springfield, and Mattie steps out on the porch to greet them. Neither Lila or Grace knows this frail woman with her graying hair neatly gathered in a snood behind her small head.

After introductions, Lila thanks Mattie for her kindness and for caring for her mother. She is surprised by the translucency of Mattie's skin and the fine web of bluish arteries beneath it. In an unguarded moment, she glances down at her own arms to see if she is aging that way, but sees only the opaque tan from her many hours under the sun. Over dinner Lila learns that Mattie's been a bookkeeper all her life.

The minister at Mattie's church has agreed to attend to the funeral rites, and Grace and Mattie read a few prepared remarks. Lila's grateful not to have been called on to talk about the mother she has not seen almost since her father's death. As her mother's pine coffin is lowered into the damp earth, Lila steps away from the graveside, afraid she'll be unable to control her sadness. She wishes Theron were by her side; for many years, she has counted on his patience, forbearance, and common sense, but she also knows that those same strengths have kept him from knowing his own sadness.

26

THE EXIGENCIES OF FARM LIFE KEEP LILA AND Theron busy. Every day there are chores to be done. Their lives and those of their animals depend on them. They buy only what they need and can afford. Each spring, when the Flats come alive again with the sound of running water, Lila and Theron resume the cycle of planting and harvest. Nature relieves them of a lot of the planting; they have only to harvest the maple, wild fruit, shang, trout, perch, morels, and venison on their land and in the unsurveyed wilderness around them. They feel an abundance in their lives that doesn't derive from the buying of things. They see some of their neighbors acquiring more modern conveniences and reveling in their ownership, while the familiar tools Lila and Theron have used over their years together have become like family—worn, but cared for, familiar, and still practical.

Theron helps Lila work the damp spring soil in her gardens as she forks in old manure he wheelbarrows over from the midden outside his barn. She plants her peas and root vegetables, while her kitchen fills up with the more fragile "starts" to be added later to the cold frames, and then to the garden beds when the frost is behind them and the soil is again warmed by the sun.

At night Theron rubs homemade unguents on Lila's arthritic hands, and Lila does the same for Theron's increasingly painful right shoulder. The repetitive arc of his bucksaw, scythe, and pitchfork wear away at his rotator cuff, and the pain in his shoulder is relieved only by Lila's gentle ministrations.

Sometimes when Theron is clearing their two dishes from the table and Lila is washing up, he'll see from behind several sudden rhythmic intakes of breath and know she has conjured the children they expected would share their chores and meals. He knows she resists these involuntary sobs that come upon her suddenly, and he knows she doesn't want to make him unhappy as well, as their early years together were filled with talk of the children they would have—how many boys, how many girls, what their names might be and whom they'd take after. Elise once suggested to Lila that she and Theron talk with Doc Jewett about the matter, but Lila and Theron know that such matters are not discussed with strangers.

When crews begin setting poles down the Flats Road in 1957 and electricity finally comes to the neighborhood, Leonard suggests an electrician to help Theron bring it into his house and barn. Theron specifies light sockets only in the kitchen, parlor and bedroom, but the electrician convinces him to wire the upstairs as well with both sockets and outlets. In the barn the electrician runs sockets above the stanchions and in the hayloft, and he convinces Theron to let him wire the milking parlor with its own circuit, explaining that the dairy co-op is about to mandate a new milk storage system and that cold boxes and milk cans will soon be obsolete.

The next time Theron goes to town to take his milk to the creamery and pick up his milk check, he goes to Morton's Hardware and buys Lila a Hyleco tabletop radio set for their forty-fifth wedding anniversary. When he returns, she's weeding in her herb garden. Theron pushes the plug into the new wall socket near the dining room table and turns the knob clockwise "past the click," as Jack Morton has shown him, and suddenly the room fills with music. Theron quickly turns down the knob and the music subsides, but the silence of their life in the Flats is broken for good. Lila comes running into the house and beams at Theron. She grabs him by the arm and begins to waltz him around the small kitchen to the strains of Woody Herman.

Other than the bustle of meal preparation, canning, preserving, the crackle of a newly set fire in the woodstove, the creaking of pine boards as Lila bustles about, or talking about the day's work while Mags purrs on his cushion by the stove, their home's been quiet for their forty-five years together. Occasionally Lila will signal with a pointed finger the scrabbling sound of mice living in the pantry walls. Theron must trust Lila, as he doesn't hear them. The several dowel plugs filling small holes where the mice have chewed through the pine baseboards are a testament to their presence. As they age together, the silence of their long life together will expand as Theron's hearing ebbs.

Just as Lila notes for him the subtle noises he cannot hear, so must she consult him when she can no longer read the hen-scratching with which she's labeled and dated all her canning jars. She jokes with Theron that as they grow old that together they'll make one whole person, with her dependence on his eyesight and his dependence on her acute hearing. Theron laughs and reminds her that, at sixty-three, he's already old. He doesn't remind her that she's older than he is, though, when they were "young and frisky," as Lila likes to say, he did once accuse her of "cradle robbin'."

The two enjoy their new radio. Lila turns it on when she gets up just before six to make breakfast and brew their coffee. During the day, the only radio station they listen to is WDEV in faraway Waterbury. A show called *The Trading Post* comes on at six, and after a brief update of milk and commodity farm prices, the announcer reads from the cards mailed into the station, detailing goods for sale or sought after: farm machinery, iceboxes, wringer washers, newborn piglets, heifers . . . an endless and intriguing commerce carried on the airwaves. Lila hears of newfangled things she doesn't recognize and regales Theron over breakfast with their descriptions.

The 1960s are a time of change. Some farmers are selling out and seeking jobs on the mountain in nearby Stowe or at the new IBM factory being built in Essex Junction. Wringer washers, condenser-topped refrigerators, and console tube radios give way to televisions, dishwashers, electric mixers, and toasters. Drawbar farm equipment sits rusting in fields as farmers buy new machinery that runs off power take-offs from the newer tractors. Hay balers replace haylifts, farm wagons, and pitchforks.

The occasional feelings of sadness that rise up in Lila catch her off guard. Although she usually assuages them through her daily work, as time goes on they linger. Theron notices these slight changes and tries to allay Lila's sadness. The comfort he sought in vain as a child comes more easily to him now in the giving of it, and his efforts always have a positive effect on Lila. She smiles at Theron, knowing how much he wants to help. But she also knows that feelings often come on without purpose or meaning and are to be endured.

Sometimes she'll harness up Norma to her old trap and make the half-hour trip over to Annie's for a visit. Apart from a budding maternal friendship with Flora, a hippie living down the road, Annie remains Lila's only close friend.

Like Theron and Lila, Annie and Beth have managed to support themselves and grow their income a bit each year to cover the ever increasing cost of staples bought in town. Over the last two years they've built a horse barn with twelve box stalls they rent out to their new, more affluent neighbors.

Annie and Lila enjoy each other's company and always find much to talk about to lift their spirits. They don't offer one another solutions to their problems but rather comfort in talking about them. The timbre of conversations between women is different from that between men; Lila always returns home feeling refreshed from her time with Annie, and Theron is grateful Lila has Annie's friendship.

A few newcomers camp and squat farther down the road, while another couple buys a few cheap acres with a hunting camp and settles in. Theron and Lila see Volkswagen "bugs" and campers for the first time. They're surprised to hear music coming from these small vehicles and to learn that radios are now standard in most cars. They like their gregarious neighbors, who drop by on occasion for advice about growing and planting or to buy Lila's preserves, vegetables, fruit, and cut flowers.

Lila especially likes Flora and her husband, who calls himself Crow. She's amused by what they wear and how they talk and is impressed by how hard they both work to eke out a living on the few damp acres they bought. Flora's in her early twenties and cultivates herbs, including marijuana, which she refers to as Mary Jane. Curious, Lila asks about the herb and what it's used for, and Flora smiles. Lila learns that its cultivation is illegal and doesn't pursue the question of its medical use, though she remains curious.

Crow harvests basswood, cedar, and pine in the nearby woods, and carves elegant raptors, owls, and nesting birds, all in various stages of movement. He has yet to develop a market for his work and is still learning the carving techniques that he hopes will make him famous some day.

In the spring, Flora stops by to seek Lila's advice on working the damp soil and starting the various culinary and medicinal herbs she grows; many of the plants Flora starts inside and transplants to her garden simply wilt and die in the wet clay soil. Lila helps her work sand, wood ash, and compost into the soil and shows Crow where to dig a drainage ditch so the garden soil can dry out. Flora shares with Lila her book learning about various herbs, and Lila adds some new varieties to her own herb garden from starts that Flora brings her. Lila shows Flora how to tie and dry her herbs and to make infusions and herbal syrups for later use.

In the fall of Flora and Crow's second year in the Flats, Flora tells Lila she's pregnant and Lila smiles, giving her a hug. Flora conveys to Lila her fears about bearing a child and Lila assures that it'll be fine, "natural as can be."

At first the news rekindles Lila's melancholy, but in time she comes to see the occasion as an opportunity to help her young neighbor. Flora asks about Lila's children, and Lila, smiling, tells her she and Theron couldn't have any. Flora doesn't press the point, and Lila invokes humor to ease Flora's embarrassment. "Guess I was born a spent hen," she says with a laugh.

Flora takes her hand. "Well, you can be our child's auntie. I would say *godmother*, but Crow and I don't believe in God."

After Theron has finished the milking, he trudges back up to the house to await the supper Lila presents with a flourish each evening; while she cooks they talk about their new neighbors and assess how the world around them is changing. Unlike some, they enjoy the changes they observe in how their neighbors live and dress and the tools and strange words they use.

After dinner Lila switches on the radio and moves the large knob slowly across the circular dial away from WDEV on the far left until she finds her favorite nighttime station, WWVA in Wheeling, West Virginia. She has come to love the hillbilly music broadcast every night, the ballads of love lost and won. They're different from the Irish- and Québécois-influenced tunes she remembers from barn dances as a child in Springfield or the logging camps where her father worked, which were for dancing, not storytelling.

Among her old-timey favorites are Bob Wills and His Texas Playboys, the Carter Family, the Blue Sky Boys, the Maddox Brothers and Rose, and Hank Williams. Sprinkled among these she also hears the likes of Chuck Berry, George Jones, and Elvis Presley, whom she finds "a bit too riled" for her taste. Of the country and western singers, she likes Johnny Cash and Marty Robbins, but her all-time new favorite is Vaughn Monroe. When the opening chords of "Ghost Riders in the Sky" begin, she shushes Theron if he's talking so she can absorb the full mystery of the song; it thrills her every time.

27

IN THE 1960s, VERY FEW HILL FARMS STILL HAUL MILK cans to a creamery. The flatbed trucks that once gathered milk cans from wooden stands at the ends of dirt roads have been replaced with refrigerated stainless steel tanker trucks that come daily to large farms or every other day to smaller ones and pump out the fresh milk stored in their tanks. Willingly or not, most farmers have committed to modern mechanized farming: new cropping machines, Surge milking units, and refrigerated stainless steel milk tanks. Others less comfortable with debt sell out, auctioning what's left, but retirement for reasons other than ill health is still rare. At the urging of the local extension agent, farmers have been switching to the new systems for several years—even though, many farmers protest, they cost as much as nine months' or even a year's worth of their milk sales.

Chester Collins, the extension agent who visits Theron a few times a year, breaks the news to him and Lila over a midafternoon cup of coffee that the new milk processor will no longer accept milk in cans and that he'll have to install the new system. He lays out the government scheme to help farmers make the transition: they pay five hundred dollars cash down and the remaining thousand dollars will be deducted from their milk checks over a period of thirty-six months.

Lila sees the familiar twitch in Theron's jaw. It is, she knows, the only signal of his fear. She comes to his rescue, telling Chester that they will have to retire from farming if the new requirement stands. Chester nods and makes clear that there are no other options for those wishing to sell milk. He thanks them for the coffee and doughnut and leaves, doffing his orange and black Surge Milker cap.

Theron is still quiet. Lila knows the sadness of unrecoverable things and people and animals. She, too, has lived through loss.

"We'll keep Gladys and Polly for our own milk and butter makin', and some for the neighbors. We'll sell the rest of the girls. Hand milkin' is hard work, and I seen how th' arthritis is twistin' up your hands. 'S time to call it quits. We got lotsa other farm work, and we can make do—always have, always will. Th' rest a' the girls'll do fine on another farm bein' among their own 'n' all."

Theron just nods his head and gets up to go outdoors. He knows she's right, but for now he needs to be alone and seek solace in his woods. He hates to have Lila see his tears. He traipses off into the pasture toward the woods with the fourth Mags trotting along behind.

Lila, standing on the porch, knows Theron's doing what he must and that he'll have his time in the glen, stroking Mags, who'll sit patiently in his lap until he's ready to return. This time, she notices, he leaves his fishing pole behind. He'll sit quietly, absorbing his sadness until he no longer fears tearing up and Lila can minister to him with her comforts.

Theron and Mags return in time to start milking. He addresses the girls quietly by name as he gently draws milk from them into the pail. Mags stands by for his squirts, and his progeny hide in the shadows waiting for their saucer.

While milking, Theron remembers his father, curled up like a child on Edna's hind haunch, speaking softly to her. He feels ashamed. Cows are dumb animals, he thinks, incapable of offering comfort to a human being. But he also knows the quiet peace he experiences when he's alone with his girls and better understands the implacable sadness his father sought to numb with drink and Edna's warmth. Lila's tenderness evokes in him his father's sense of loss and loneliness.

Theron never drinks. As the memory of his father's despair at losing his mother and his own despair at losing his father to drink returns, he pauses in his milking. He's grateful to be alone in the cool barn. He finishes milking Lisa, empties the pail into a milk can in the spring box and then climbs the ladder to the loft to fork down hay. The change in the order of his habitual chores is calming. Mags looks at him from a nearby windowsill, confused at the change.

When a forkful of hay lies below each water bowl, Theron finishes milking, pours a cup of milk in the saucer in the corner, calls to Mags, and the two return to the house where Lila knows not to ask how he's doing. She knows he's okay and always will be. Over their many years together, Lila's come to understand her husband better, and loves him more each day.

28

AFTER CONSULTING WITH HIS FRIEND WILLARD, Theron sends a note to Willis Hicks, a local cattle auctioneer in Cady's Falls, explaining that he wants to sell his herd privately and knows he'll take less for it. Hicks has heard this before. Auctions can be a prelude to penury and dependence on others or to idleness and decline. Few lifelong dairymen are able to imagine a life worth living after their years tending animals and working fields. It's often said that death scouts farm auctions.

Mr. Hicks visits Theron and tells him he has a client in East Berkshire who's building his herd out to six hundred head, a number unfathomable to Theron.

"Betcha 'em girls don' 'ave no names," Theron mutters, "plastic earrings is all."

"Right 'bout that," Hicks answers. "I'll get 'im ta come 'n' take a look at yer girls and give you a number. He's a fair man, won' rob ya like some'll do. I'll tell ya if the number's fair. Yer Uncle Adrian was m' teacher in tenth grade. Din't learn much, but it wasn't his fault. Never did learn much. All I knows is cows. Knows 'em well enough by now, I s'pose."

Two weeks later Mr. Hicks and Alphonse Choinière arrive unannounced, as Theron and Lila still have no phone. "Who's gonna call us, anyway?" Lila asks Rena LeClaire when she urges her to have a phone installed.

Mr. Choinière speaks some English, but his Québécois accent makes it necessary for Mr. Hicks to parlay the final deal with Theron and Lila. Theron's surprised at the offer and nods his assent, as does Lila. Hicks assures him the offer's fair, and the deal's concluded with a handshake.

Two weeks later two Chevy pickups hauling aluminum cattle trailers drive on to the grass and park in tandem by the barn. It takes two trips from the Flats to East Berkshire to transport Theron and Lila's herd.

As they load the first girls into the trailer, Lila sees the familiar twitch in Theron's jaw. She knows another piece of his life is gone. When one of the handlers starts hitting a recalcitrant Guernsey repeatedly on her rear flank with his cane, Theron starts to speak up; Lila takes his hand quietly to calm him. She knows Theron has never used a prod on an animal. When he needs to urge one of his girls forward, he does so with a gentle hand and a firm word.

When both trailers are loaded and underway, Lila nods toward the kitchen. Theron walks behind her so she can't see the tears in his eyes. Theron slumps in his chair and Lila slices some pork and bread, slathering the bread with pork fat and her pickle relish. She pours them each a glass of her tomato juice and sits down next to Theron. Their family is smaller now, and the days will seem longer to them.

With the chainsaw, a gas can, a jug of chain oil, a double-bitted axe, and a peavey in the bucket of his tractor, Theron leaves each morning to cut firewood, going ever deeper into the Flats to find maple, oak, ash, beech, birch, and hickory. The pulp wood market is gone, but with the influx of hippies and do-it-yourself home builders, woodstoves are making a comeback. Wood boilers appear alongside rural homes, and the market for seasoned firewood is growing.

Now in his early eighties, Theron feel his limits. His hours wrestling the cranky chainsaw and stacking wood in his old hay wagon shrink to about four or five each day.

Try as he might, on the rare occasions when the chainsaw won't start, he's unable to fathom its mysteries and has to take the buggy into Morton's to have them tinker it back to life. While his mechanic cleans the air filter, flushes the carburetor, and installs a new spark plug, Jack Morton tells Theron one of his legendary stories.

"Did ya 'ear the one 'bout the Canuck logger?" asks Jack. Since his own logging days, Theron has rarely been in the company of men.

"French Canuck logger walks into ma' store and asks me ta sharpen his two-man saw. Surprised, I ask 'im if he's ever used a chainsaw. 'What's dat?' he says. I show him one and he scoffs, 'Too 'eavy, eh?' So I ask him how many cords he cuts in a week.''Bout twenty,' he answers.

"I tell 'im ta take the saw for a week while I sharpen his handsaw and keep track a' how many cords he cuts with it. 'You come back, and if you haven't cut fifty, I'll give ya the saw at half price,' I tell 'im.

"Week later, the Canuck returns, shakin' his head and tellin' me he wants his handsaw back. I ask 'im how many cords he cut. ''Bout six,' he answers.

"'Wait a minute,' I say, 'That's impossible. Somethin' must be wrong. Chain's brand new on this baby.' The saw starts up on my first pull. Canuck jumps back and says, 'Wha's dat noise?'"

Laughter breaks out around the store among the customers who've stopped to listen. Theron laughs too, although he wonders if on some level he's not the object of the joke.

Though he's best in the morning, Theron no longer has to rise at four thirty. But old habits die hard, and Lila sometimes hears Theron stacking wood before dawn. He joins Lila at noon for lunch and then takes a nap in his chair. He continues cropping hay, but the market for loose hay is gone. A few horse owners stop by and fill their pickups and trailers, but now people pay earnest money only for square bales.

. . .

The following year Theron makes a deal with Wayne Frenette in Elmore to bale his hay in exchange for half of it. Theron then sells his share of the bales to what he calls the horsey set, and they pay more than farmers.

Lila's eyesight is getting worse, and she can no longer read. The screech of Theron's chainsaw diminishes what little's left of his hearing, but he doesn't connect the two, assuming old age is simply taking its toll. Now that Lila can no longer read, he reads to her every evening in bed. Lila chooses books from the library, and Theron always enjoys her choices. The one exception is MacKinlay Kantor's *Andersonville*, which was recommended by the new librarian in Morristown. Neither Lila nor Theron had any idea of the savagery of the Civil War. The mystery of Uncle Adrian's descent into madness after serving overseas becomes clearer as Lila and Theron read of the horrors their countrymen experienced in the only war that took place on their own soil.

One day Lila slips coming up the stairs to the porch and injures her knee. Her left shin swells up and becomes discolored and Theron knows he must take her to be seen by Dr. Hyle, who's taken over Doc Jewett's practice since he retired.

Theron leaves word in his mailbox for Rena to come by. He's not fond of Rena and finds her "nosy and questionin',", but she has become their link to the rare services they need as age erodes their independence.

Rena comes by the following day and drives Lila and Theron to Dr. Hyle's office in Morristown. The doc tells Lila she has dermatitis and that it's serious if unchecked. Theron thinks he hears "mastitis," and looks at Lila questioningly.

"Speak up," she tells him.

"How does a woman git mastitis? Thought only cows got that."

The doc and Lila have a good laugh at Theron's expense, until Lila lets him in on the joke. At first, Theron looks hurt, then smiles. Dr. Hyle prescribes penicillin, tablets that he shakes into an envelope from his own supply, and he scribbles the dosage directions on the outside of the envelope. Aware of her diminishing eyesight, he instructs them both that she is to take one capsule four times a day with a glass of water.

Because of her eyesight and some tingling she mentions in her legs, Dr. Hyle tells Lila he wants to take a urine sample and sends her into the toilet with a small glass jar. Several days later, he stops by the farm and tells Lila she has "the sugar." He explains what this means and what precautions she must take to avoid its deadly effects. Diabetes, he explains, is causing her declining eyesight and a loss of feeling in her feet. Lila has known women who got the sugar and knows there are those who take care of themselves and give up sweet pastries, and then there's those who can't and make no effort to forestall the disease's progress. She's not one of these, she tells Theron; she's going to take her condition seriously and enjoy the fruits and vegetables she's always raised.

Theron now understands why he's seen Lila's outstretched hand groping for a kitchen implement or how she burns herself reaching for a pan on the wood-stove. He pointedly asks her what she can see and, reluctantly, she admits to him she sees little beyond shapes and shadows.

29

LILA AND THERON HAVE LIVED MOST OF THEIR LIVES in the Flats, coming out occasionally to the Elmore Store to trade for necessities. Lila is now ninety-three, and Theron ninety-one. Lila didn't get "the sugar" early like her friend Annie, who suffers from terrible dropsy. Lila was diagnosed at eighty-nine. Except for a few skin cancers, a locked-up shoulder, and deafness, Theron has kept his health. He grows cut flowers and root vegetables to sell at the Morrisville farmer's market or to aging hippies who sometimes come to Lila and Theron's ramshackle house to buy them right out of the stone-lined root cellar, where they're available year-round.

Rena LeClaire, the Morristown home health nurse, has been troubled for some time over Theron's steadfast rejection of her services. She takes great pride in the care she provides for the town's seniors; last year she was cited by the county for her "conscientious service" to seniors living at home, though it was suggested by some that she contributed to the economic demise of Copley Manor, the town home for dependent seniors.

To Rena's dismay and hurt, Theron rejects her services outright. Theron tells her he "don' want ya snoopin' roun' my house lookin' for vi'lations an' the like." Rena's not accustomed to such out-and-out rejection. Occasionally she encounters reticence on the part of a senior or family member that she attributes to modesty, Yankee independence, or pride, but she usually prevails, patiently explaining that she's only there to help out and does so only to the extent her charge is willing. Most of the seniors on her route look forward to her care and company, as she brings mail, tidbits of local gossip, and even light groceries if called in advance. While there she changes bed linens, runs a load of wash if there's a machine, discards old food, bathes those in her care and, with great authority, checks their vitals. One of Rena's charges, who's hard of hearing and keeps the hearing aid she brought him in the icebox "so the batt'ries don' run down," hears "vittles" instead of "vitals" and insists he has plenty to eat, then lets her check his pulse and blood pressure.

Lila's diabetes progresses quickly. Over the years she's put on some weight; but it has collected over the years like a retirement plan – evenly muscled due to the steady routine of her chores and helping Theron.

Eventually word gets around that a diabetic stroke has left Lila incapable of speech and partially paralyzed. This bit of news heightens Rena's sense of urgency about Lila and Theron. She suspects things aren't right in their home and that Theron may have sinister reasons for denying her access to Lila.

She starts up her rusty Subaru wagon and heads up Route 12 toward Elmore, turning off just north of the lake and bouncing along the Flats Road until the turnoff that leads deeper into the puckerbrush and Theron and Lila's homestead. She pulls into the dirt driveway, sets the parking brake, and waits a minute as she always does to give people a chance to gather themselves before she knocks on the door. Theron's just coming in from the woodpile with an armload of wood for the cookstove. A bright sun shines through the clouds. He spots Rena and walks purposefully over to her car before she can get out, setting the firewood down hard on the hood of her car and peering into the closed car window. Unable to get out, she rolls down her window and begins, "Now see here . . ."

"No need to git out. Y' ain' stayin' and I ain' visitin'. We'se doin' fine wi'out ya'."

"Theron, I'm not here to see you. I came to see Lila. She's a sick woman, and it's my job to take care of her and see to it that she gets medical care."

"She's been to th' 'ospital. They sent her home and told me ta care for her, and I do."

"You can't. You don't know how. Lila's diabetic. She needs special care."

"I give's 'er her sugar medicine and see's to her. Now git."

"Theron, I don't know what you're hiding, but I am coming back with the sheriff."

"Bes' bring two, ya ol' bitch. Now *git*!"

Rena drives off down the dirt road, her chin high and her hands tight on the steering wheel, which seems to have a mind of its own in the muddy ruts of the thawing road.

The more Rena thinks about it, the more her instincts tell her that Theron's hiding something to do with Lila. Folks often resist the idea of someone from outside "doing for them." Even after seven years, Rena herself still spends a good hour tidying up her own modest home before Vi, her cleaning lady, comes. Rena doesn't want it bruited about town that she keeps an untidy home, and Vi's a gossip.

Theron's overt hostility clearly indicates to Rena that he's hiding something. She's seen enough in her lifetime of service to suspect men who are secretive, and to fear that physical abuse might be the reason. Occasionally the fatigue and resentment of caring for someone day in and day out can erupt into abuse.

She remembers that some time back Theron had a run-in with the game warden for jacking deer on his own property. Theron had claimed that he and Lila needed the meat. The confrontation escalated into a tussle, after which the warden sported a black eye. No charges were ever brought, and Theron was more discreet thereafter. But clearly, Rena reasons, Theron has it in him to strike out.

She drives straight to see Willard Sanders, who runs the county's social welfare office in Morristown. Willard is known as a fair man. You can't put one over him—he can differentiate between sloth and need and isn't afraid to do so—but he also understands the stress and indignity that poverty places on families. It's in his nature to treat those in his care with respect, and he makes sure Rena does as well. His father's older sister died in the county poor farm.

Thursday afternoons at four, Rena reports to him on her service visits, noting any changes in health, family problems, or household issues. Sometimes folks run out of wood before winter runs out of cold or well lines freeze up, leaving them without water.

By the time she gets there, Rena's worked up a strong case that Lila's at grave risk of violence from her husband, whose rabid behavior made clear that something's not right in the household. "I think that crazy old goat is beating her!" she exclaims, and it takes Willard several minutes to calm her down.

Willard listens calmly, asks a few questions, and promises to follow up with a visit of his own the following day. This does little to calm Rena, and she urges that they return together immediately to rescue Lila.

"Theron and Lila have survived seventy years together. Another day isn't going to make a difference," says Willard with calm finality.

Shaking her head, Rena leaves Willard's office. After a reheated meatloaf supper, she checks her party line until she gets a dial tone. She dials her network of chatter-biddies to try to garner support for her assessment of the danger Lila's in.

"Willard's going up tomorrow. Won't take me, thinks it may be too dangerous," she tells Gert, a nurse friend of hers who lives in Morristown Corners. "Lila may be blind now, God knows, stroke left her part paralyzed. The old fool probably doesn't even know she needs a special diet. Probably feeds her candy bars. Even if he don't abuse her, he's probably killing her out of ignorance. It just troubles me. He won't let me near the house. He's hiding something, I just know it."

The next day the sun burns through the clouds by ten in the morning and the sky's a radiant blue. The air is still crisp, but spring is definitely in the air. Sugar makers are hard at it, driving their teams or tractors through the woods collecting sap in sledge-mounted, galvanized tanks.

Willard starts up to the Flats in his Plymouth, trying to reconcile Rena's urgent report with what he knows of Theron and Lila. The couple has never asked for help from his office and, as far as he knows, keep a modest household supported by sales from Theron's gardens and woodlot. Although determined to discover the truth of Rena's report, Willard feels little apprehension as he follows the rutted roads deeper into

Hardwood Flats. The sun blazes down as the road winds into the endless stand of boggy alders and the rich smell of earth melting and water running again lifts his spirits. It's been a long winter.

Willard remembers hunting here as a kid with his friend Eddy Bates, and getting lost, finally finding their way to a large fire in a nearby logging camp at dusk, having to spend the night there, and following a new road out to Elmore the following morning.

Willard doesn't pull into Theron's yard, but drives farther down the road, parks, and walks back to Theron's. He climbs the uneven cinder-block steps to the slightly crooked porch and knocks on the screen door. He hears footsteps inside and Theron comes to the door.

"What ya want, Willard?" asks Theron. "Veggies? Flowers won' be ready fer 'nother six weeks, at least."

"Came to inquire about how you and Lila's getting on," says Willard, looking Theron in the eye.

"Good enough," allows Theron. "That nosey bitch Rena send ya?"

"No, I come on my own," says Willard gently. "It's been a long, cold winter and some folk is jes' havin' a hard time of it and I been checkin' on a few of 'em."

"You join that newfangled church what haunts people wi' their home preachin'?"

"No, I come from town, and I'se jes' seein' ta folks. How you and Lila doin'? I know Lila suffers from the sugar."

Willard's calm tone of voice and willingness to look him in the eye allay Theron's suspicion of his old friend's reason for visiting, and he invites Willard in off the porch. He points to a rocker next to the Glenwood and slides the enameled coffeepot left so it sits directly over the firebox. Willard settles in, comfortable with the long silence.

"Jes' tell me what you wanna know, and don't beat 'round the bush," says Theron quietly, setting a mug of black coffee and a mayonnaise jar full of sugar in front of Willard on the cooler edge of the stove.

"I heard Lila suffered a stroke, and it must be hard caring for her 'n' all. Can she git 'round? She lose her speech?"

"We make do well 'nough. She can't walk, shuffles a bit. I gots ta hold her up. She lets me know how she's feelin' by smilin' or frownin'. That's 'bout it since she suffered the sugar shock."

"When you tend your greenhouses and gardens, does she stay in the house alone?" Willard asks, stirring some sugar into his coffee and looking up at Theron.

"I put 'er in the bucket," answers Theron, sipping his own coffee.

"The bucket?"

"The bucket on my tractor. C'mere, I'll show ya."

Willard rises to follow Theron out the back door toward a ragtag array of greenhouses made of scavenged windows and old framing lumber. Theron's tractor is parked near a cold frame, its bucket loader four feet off the ground. The bucket's wrapped in an old tarp, tied neatly with bailing twine. Theron unties the tarp and pulls it away, folds it and sets it on the tractor seat. In the bucket loader lies an old mattress on a thick bed of dry hay. At each end lie old couch pillows.

"I rigged this up for Lila 'cause she likes to be with me when I'se workin'. I lays 'er down on the porch and roll 'er onta the mattress, then cover 'er up with her momma's quilt and some feather pillows. I gets 'er comf'table, and she smiles; I know she likes it. I use these leather straps to make sure she don' fall out when she shifts 'round. Then I lifts 'er up high and drive 'er to wherever I'se workin'—sometimes the garden, sometimes the greenhouse, or the root cellar." She likes being where I'se at."

Willard just stares at the contraption. "Looks mighty comfortable to me," he allows.

"'Tis! I tried it m'self. After a while, Lila'll doze off in the sun and I wakes 'er wi' my special home-made tomata juice she likes so much. Weather's nice like today, we have lunch where I'se workin'."

"I know you're a busy man, Theron, and spring's comin' on fast, so I'll be on my way. If you ever need anything, please call on me."

"No phone, but I can get them ol' hippies down the road to call. Thanks for comin'. Try ta keep that bitch Rena from comin' 'round. She's al'ays lookin' fer trouble, e'en if there ain' none to be had."

"I will," promises Willard.

30

O N A COOL FALL DAY, LILA IS LYING IN THE TRACTOR bucket watching Theron pick wild apples. He has wrapped her in an extra Johnson Woolen Mills plaid blanket and tied a knit scarf around her head. She smiles as she watches her husband filling bushel baskets with green rust-dappled apples he will use to make the sour jelly, lightly sweetened with maple syrup, that she so enjoys.

After Theron heaves the second basket up onto the small wood wagon attached to the back of the tractor, he unscrews his dented thermos and pours Lila a cup of the hot chicken broth he made the day before from a scrawny hen he saw no reason to feed through the winter.

"Warm enough, honey?" he asks Lila as he brings the dented enamel cup to her lips. Theron knows his wife can't respond, but he sees answers in her eyes— a twinkle, a frown, or hint of a smile he understands as clearly as anything she might say.

A few months earlier, Dr. Hyle removed three toes on her left foot. Theron, now ninety-three, provides for them both with his various garden projects in the nearby clearings and the modest Social Security check they receive each month.

It's clear as he places his hand on her forehead that Lila is cold. She sips a bit of the chicken broth, but most runs out the side of her lips onto the feather pillow in the tractor bucket. Theron knows something's wrong. He starts up the tractor and heads for home with two bushels of wild apples and a third basket still empty.

He raises the front loader until it's flush with the porch floor and drives right up against the front porch steps. He hits the kill switch on the John Deere and climbs the steps. Theron gathers Lila to him in her quilt and blanket, pulling her gently into the warm kitchen. He feeds three maple splits into the cookstove through the large top burner and lifts Lila up onto the daybed near the stove. He sees her wince as he lays her down.

"Y'okay, honey?" he asks, noticing a wrinkle in her brow and a tremor in her left hand as he tucks the blanket around her. He sees the fear in her eyes and again offers her some broth, but she pulls her head away. He worries she's afraid, trapped inside a body, unable to respond. Initially her stroke hadn't prevented them from enjoying their time together or even from communicating with expressions of delight, surprise, or dismay, but that is no longer the case.

Theron knows Lila has taken a turn for the worse, but he decides to wait until the next day to take her to the hospital, so as not to importune the doctors and nurses who would be leaving the hospital to go home to their own families at this late hour.

The next morning, when Theron calls Willard to drive him and Lila to the hospital, he knows she's dying, though little's changed since yesterday when she was in the tractor bucket watching him pick apples.

On the trip from Hardwood Flats to Copley Hospital, Lila seems listless. Her eyes are closed and her head bobs against the window as Willard makes his way slowly along the rutted dirt road leading to Route 12.

When they arrive, Willard goes to the hospital's main entrance and asks for help bringing Lila inside. He is directed to the emergency entrance around back, where an orderly and a nurse pushing a wheelchair are already waiting. Theron and the orderly settle Lila into the wheelchair, but only Theron sees the grimace on her lips and the fear in her eyes as she looks at him. Lila is put in the same room she recovered in after her "shock" and then again when Dr. Hyle amputated three of her toes. Willard must take his leave and promises to check in in the morning.

Never taking his eyes off of Lila's face, Theron stands by, holding her hand as they wait for Dr. Hyle. The image of the tall young girl entering his homeroom in high school as a new transfer student and, then, the close-up of her face when she surprised him with his first kiss at the sugar-on-snow party come back to him. This same sweetness radiates within the wrinkled and leathery face watching from the hospital bed, but he now sees fear below the faint smile of gratitude as he holds her hand. Theron looks away only once, when Dr. Hyle enters the room.

"How's our Lila today?" the doc asks in his familiar bedside manner, and Theron sees a faint smile appear on Lila's face. Dr. Hyle orders blood and urine tests and looks carefully at Lila's feet. A nurse joins him and begins taking a blood sample.

"I'm going to have to catheterize Lila," the doc says to Theron; then he turns to the nurse, Martha, and asks her to get on it as soon as she finishes drawing blood.

Looking at Lila, Theron sees terror and abruptly interrupts the doctor.

"We'se not doin' all 'em things, Doc," Theron says, to the surprise of the nurse and doctor.

"If it's time for my Lila ta go, we ain't gonna make it harder for her by pokin' her wi' needles and tappin' her like a sugar maple. You give 'er sumpin' to make her comf'table and I'se gonna stay here 'n' hold 'er hand. Now, git 'less I call ya."

"But Theron, we don't know how sick she is and won't know unless I do some tests. You wouldn't want her leaving you before she's ready."

"She's ready. She told me so."

"But she hasn't spoken in fourteen months. How do you know for sure?"

175

"She talks to me wi' her eyes. It's clear."

A look of relief floods Lila's face and a hint of a smile appears.

"See here?" Theron says. "She's relieved. I can tell."

Martha returns shortly with a hypodermic needle, and Lila looks agitated when she sees it. Martha rolls back Lila's flannel shirt, holds her arm firmly, and administers the shot quickly.

"You best be gentle wi' my woman. She's been good to me all 'ese years," Theron warns.

"Sometimes it's best to give shots quickly before the patient knows what's happening and tenses the muscle . . . only makes it hurt more," Martha explains.

"That's good, I trust you, if'n you say so. You and Dr. Hyle al'ays been good to Lila and me, and fair 'n' all. I jes' don't want Lila all agitated when you and I both know she's leavin' us."

"I understand, Theron. You've taken good care of Lila all these years, I know that. I'm gonna leave you two to be with one another tonight, and we'll see how Lila's faring in the morning. Then we can talk about making her comfortable and whether or not to take some tests to determine how bad her sugar is. I suspect her kidneys are failing. Theron, I'll see you in the morning. You get some sleep, ya hear?"

Dr. Hyle and Martha leave the room. Theron looks back at Lila, who is sleeping peacefully, but breathing erratically. "Don' know what they gave ya, but ya sure look peaceful. Sleep well. I'll be here with ya."

Theron pulls a folding chair over by Lila's bedside and sits down. After shooing away a candy striper trying to serve Lila a plate containing nothing Theron recognizes, he too falls asleep, holding Lila's hand.

Theron wakes around four thirty as it's getting dark. Lila's hand feels cooler and he massages it gently. She opens her eyes and smiles when she sees him. He brushes a wisp of hair away from her eyes and pats her cheek. The clear skin that so entranced him as a young man is still clear, but has aged to a pale parchment under which he sees bluish veins. The eyes that so sparkled with light and excitement when Theron brought Lila home for the first time to his modest farm on the Flats are viscous and yellow now.

"You been cryin', honey? There's no need. I'se right here and ain't goin' nowheres." He sees a faint glimmer of a smile as he looks into the eyes that have long since taken up the work of her mouth and lips.

Around six thirty, Martha returns to give Lila another shot and, under the watchful eyes of Theron, proceeds very gently, rolling back Lila's sleeve and gently massaging her forearm before inserting the needle.

"Can you tell 'em we don' want no food?" asks Theron.

"Yes," Martha answers. "Sure you don't want a plate for yourself?"

"I'd take an apple if you have one, but I ain't hungry beyond that."

"One apple comin' up. They're fresh in from the Westphal orchard up yer way."

"Jerry grows good apples," Theron says as Martha leaves, closing the door behind her.

Theron pulls the chair up to the bed and watches Lila as she again falls into a deep sleep. He is adrift in his memories of their times together as a young couple, working to make their way. They had no neighbors they could depend on, and often talked at suppertime about what they could raise for sale, what they would need to trade for in town, and what they could grow in the short season on their hard-scrabble land.

He remembers watching Lila toiling in the garden and how he'd get excited and how lying in bed at night after supper, the images of her would come back and incite him to touch her. He thought of how the many times they'd made love never brought them the children they'd both dreamed of raising.

Sometime in the night, when all the sounds of the busy hospital go quiet, Theron hears—first in a dream, and then as it wakes him—a low moan from Lila. It scares him into a sudden awakening, as he has heard nothing from her until now. The noise ends just as suddenly but she, too, is awake now, again with that look of fear.

"What's wrong, honey? You okay?"

Lila's eyes close slowly and he reaches for her hand, the coolness of which surprises him. He pulls the blankets up to her chin and over their held hands.

She seems to relax somewhat and he wonders if she too has been dreaming.

"I wanted to tell you my sorrowfuls," Theron begins.

Lila opens her eyes again.

"I'se sorry for the times I'se away from you, going to town, the time I had to take work at the lumber mill to earn us money for winter stores, the time Adrian died and I was gone for so long, the times I spent up on the mountain when I couldn't get the sadness out of me."

He looks into her eyes for a sign of forgiveness.

"I'se sorry for not giving you the children we both wanted. We was never lonely in each other's company, but I know how much we both wanted kids to raise and work together in our gardens. I'se most sorry about that. I could see in your eyes you wantin' little ones too.

"I'se sorry 'bout the hard winters we spent together. Seems like no matter how hard we worked, some falls we just couldn't put up enough to get through 'em winters and that time I had to take credit in town, which we both promised never to do, 'cause it would get us off wrong come spring.

"I'se sorry for my long bouts of sadness and the times I'd go all silent and you'd try so hard to bring me comfort, but I couldn't be comforted no matter, and I'd have to jes' get through the sadness by myself, knowing it would go away and you'd be there and not be harsh on me 'n' all. I've always had the sadness in me, but you was always there. You was patient for me.

"I know you coulda had a better life in town or with someone who'd a done better 'n' all, but I did the best I knew to do. Maybe I din't know all the hows and whys of life, but I always loved you best I could in my ways."

The following morning Martha comes in at six. Theron is lying next to Lila in the hospital bed, holding her hand. Martha finds no vital signs in Lila and Theron is breathing peacefully.

Theron wakes up when he hears Martha calling out arrangements in the hall. He rises from Lila's side and kisses her slowly on the lips as Dr. Hyle enters the room. Martha informs him that Lila has "passed" in the night.

"No, she died," Theron says. Then he thanks them both and leaves, telling Dr. Hyle, "Take good care of my Lila. I'll be back for her tomorrow."

31

T HE NEXT MORNING THERON IS WAITING AT THE
front door of the hospital. He imagines the hospital to be like the few stores at which he trades, opening at 8:00 a.m. and closing at 5:00 p.m., so when he sees the clock over the reception desk reach eight o'clock, he pushes open the glass door and enters, approaching the desk and saying to the desk clerk, "I'se here to pick up Lila and bring her home."

The clerk scans a clipboard on the side of her desk.

"I am so sorry to tell you, sir, that Mrs. Wright died the day before yesterday during the night. Did no one here manage to reach you?"

"I know she's dead, I was lyin' wi' 'er upstairs when she died. I'se jes' here to take 'er home. Dr. Hyle'll know. He here yet?"

"He gets in at nine, but let me call our social services director, Claire Couture. I'm sure she'll be able to help you."

"No need to trouble 'er. I'll jes' wait 'til Dr. Hyle comes. Jes' tell 'im I'se here waitin' on him. I'll be right here."

Keeping her eyes on the strange man pacing in the lobby, the clerk surreptitiously picks up the re-

181

ceiver and calls Claire's office down the hall, whispering into the phone about an elderly man pacing in the lobby looking to pick up his deceased wife.

Small rural hospitals manage all kinds of medical emergencies and personal urgencies. The economic spectrum runs the gamut from well-heeled patients arriving by ambulance from the ski slopes and chalets of Stowe to those arriving in pickups from the tiny hamlets and trailer parks of Eden, Wolcott, Elmore, Belvidere, and Woodbury. Patients with nonstandard ailments are directed to Claire's office. Over her many years she's learned the diversity of woes that cause people to seek help: an elderly man dodging his approaching death because he hasn't been able to make arrangements for his dog after he dies; a widow living in her trailer who lost her dentures and then her glasses and can't afford to replace either one; an uncle who hasn't spoken for several months . . . the list goes on. A multitude of troubles can arise in the hills and hollows of tiny towns where poverty is rife and state and federal relief services are slim or suspect.

Claire enters the waiting area and recognizes Theron from his time at the hospital when Lila had her stroke and from the time Dr. Hyle operated on her. Recognizing Claire, Theron agrees to follow her to her office until Dr. Hyle arrives.

"Bankers' hours, I guess," Theron mutters, shaking his head. "'Bout this time I'se thinkin' on lunch. Folks don't seem to know much 'bout work these days."

"Dr. Hyle works hard enough," Claire asserts as they walk down the tiled corridor. "Just last Friday, he was here all night. We had a flurry of folks in, and his relief doctor has to come all the way from Burlington. I've seen him work eighteen hours without stopping, except for a coffee on the run. Can get mighty busy here, 'specially in the fall and before Christmas."

"I know he's a good man. I din't mean no disparaging by it. He took good care of my Lila the two times she 'as here and he sewed up my hand once and din't charge me nothing, so I brung 'im four quarts a' wild blueberries and a jug a' syrup for his troubles."

Claire settles in behind her desk, and Theron sits on the edge of a chair on the other side.

"So you're going to bury your Lila. I am sorry she's gone. Good woman, Lila was."

"She was a good woman, and I wanna do right by 'er in her dying. I'se gonna bury 'er myself in her favorite spot where we use ta have our picnics down by the brook below the berry patches. I saved up some a' ma cut flowers 'n' all. I'se gonna treat her right, like she treated me all 'er life.

"We ain' never been churchy folks, ya see. Never asked much of other folks. Sometimes, we'd jes' think together on those folks with nothin', livin' like animals in the forest and we'd live thankful, like 'ey do."

Claire sees moisture in Theron's eyes. "Just so you know, let me tell you your choices under the law."

"Don't care 'bout no law. I cares 'bout ma Lila."

"I know that, Theron, but we both want to do this right so there's no trouble like you had with Rena."

"That cow better steer clear a' me and Lila!"

"She won't be anywhere around. Don't worry about Rena."

"Lila can be buried in the Elmore Cemetery, or you can bury her at home. She doesn't have to be embalmed, but she must be buried within three days of her death if you choose not to. It's not legal to transport a dead person yourself, but Dr. Hyle and I will overlook you bringing Lila home yourself. Dr. Hyle has already filled out the death certificate and necessary papers, so we can release Lila to you today, but you have to promise us both that you'll bury her tomorrow, wherever you choose—and I know you know how to do that."

Theron seems far away. During Claire's set speech, she notices his head hanging lower and suddenly his chest heaves with a heavy sob.

"She 'as such a good woman. Don't know what I'll do wi'out her. She and I'se been together over seventy years, and now she's gone. I know ta take care a' myself . . . have well 'nough since she had her sugar stroke, but now I don't knows I wanna, with her gone and all." Theron breaks down in deep sobs and tries to catch his breath. Claire comes around her desk and puts her hand on Theron's shoulder as he weeps freely into his hands.

After several quiet minutes a knock on the door prompts Theron to pull his handkerchief from his back pocket, wipe his eyes, and blow his nose.

"Morning, Theron," Dr. Hyle says. "I thought maybe I'd see you yesterday, but we've been taking good care of Lila. I got all her paperwork done, and I bet Claire's already explained your options to you. She's good at that."

Sensing Theron is not yet ready to talk, Claire explains to Dr. Hyle that Theron will be burying Lila himself at home.

"She explained the rules . . . you can do as you please. I didn't get a chance to say much when you left yesterday morning, but I'm truly sorry Lila's gone."

"Me, too, Doc, terrible sorry. Missin' her already."

"I'm sure you are. You'll need to take care of yourself in the next few months, especially with winter coming on. You all ready, got your wood up and stores in?"

"Mostly," answers Theron, blowing his nose again.

Claire phones Willard and asks for his help bringing Lila and Theron back to the Flats. He arrives fifteen minutes later. She then phones an orderly to bring Lila to the emergency room entrance and to help Theron lay her out in the back seat of Willard's sedan.

Dr. Hyle and Claire wave good-bye to Theron as Willard drives off.

Claire takes the afternoon off to drive out to Hardwood Flats to let a few of Theron's closer neighbors know that Lila's died and to ask them to check in on him. The trip is necessary, as few of his neighbors yet have phones—locals or hippies—though they all know Theron and Lila.

When she's made her rounds, she stops at Theron's to check in on him. He isn't there, but Lila's lying on her daybed near the cookstove. A freshly made pine box is propped up near the porch window. A milk pail full of fresh-cut flowers stands in the corner and a large pile of dried flowers is on the kitchen table.

As Claire turns to leave, she sets an envelope on the table—cash she's authorized to dispense for folks in dire need. It's only forty dollars, but it will be significant to Theron, who buys little more than gas for his old truck, tractor, and chainsaw, kerosene for his lamps, spring seeds, flour, cooking oil, salt, sugar, and coffee.

As she steps off the porch she sees Theron coming and waves to him. When he reaches the porch, he asks Claire, "Wanna see where I'se gonna bury my Lila?"

"I'd like that," Claire answers, and follows Theron down the hill along a fern-lined path through a thicket of ash and hickory to the brook that runs along the east boundary of his property and, farther down, forms the glen, Theron's favorite spot.

They soon arrive at a moss-covered slope along the edge of the brook. A wide grave stands on the upper slope surrounded by more cut daylilies, dahlias, monkshood, black-eyed susans, and anemones and a cluster of fruiting choke-cherry branches. Among the flowers sit four mason jars of Theron's venison mincemeat.

"I'se gonna sit wi' 'er tonight and then bring her down in her bucket and lay 'er ta rest tomorrow, mid-day, when the sun's highest."

"You want any visitors for when you bury Lila?" Claire asks.

"No, I best be alone, not sure I can be civil. Sad, don' ya know . . . overcomes me sometime. Best if I be alone, but thanks for offerin'."

Claire follows Theron back to the house, says her good-byes, and drives back to the hospital, where the needs of other folks have piled up in her message box.

Theron spends the night talking with his Lila, reminiscing on their travails and joys together. He holds her hand for much of the evening and keeps the fire burning as he knows how she dislikes being cold.

Late the next morning he brings the tractor around to the front and prepares it for her last ride. He shakes the dead stink bugs and wasps out of the old mattress, wraps her in her mother's crazy quilt, and fluffs up her feather pillow. He then drives the tractor up to the front porch and brings Lila out, laying her out as he always has in her bucket. Then he props the pine coffin up on the drawbar, leans it against the back of the tractor seat, and sets off down the path to Lila's burial site.

At the brook's edge he climbs down and lays out two manila ropes parallel to one another on the ground near the dug grave and sets the coffin over them. He then lowers the bucket so he can lift Lila off and lay her in the pine coffin. When he has arranged her comfortably, he sets two mason jars of mincemeat in the coffin on either side of her, places a bouquet of his black dahlias on her breast, kisses her good-bye and sits down on the moss and weeps.

After some time Theron recovers himself, lifts the coffin cover in place, and nails it shut with eighteen finishing nails he has in his overalls pocket. He then ties the ropes around the hydraulic arms of the loader, lifts Lila's coffin off the moss with the tractor, and inches forward until the coffin hangs over the newly dug grave. Then he slowly lowers Lila in, turns off the tractor, dismounts, pulls the ropes out from under the coffin, and sits down on the moss, where he again begins to sob.

After several minutes Theron thinks he hears someone coming down the path and turns to see his friend, Willard Sanders, limping slowly through the ferns.

"Hello, Theron, thought maybe you could use some company while you laid Lila to her rest. I just heard from Dr. Hyle that you was buryin' 'er today, and I thought I'd come see you and say g'bye ta 'er, too, and see how you'se farin'." Willard surveys the area, then adds, "You dig that all by yer lonesome? That's a lot a work for a man yer age. I'm too old now ta help, but I coulda got you some help."

"I done it okay."

Willard sits down next to Theron, and the two talk for some time about the days when they were young and just starting out to make their way in the world.

Finally Theron gets to his feet, gathers up the rest of his flowers, and drops them onto the coffin. With the help of his walking stick, Willard clambers up and stands by as Theron starts the tractor and begins backfilling the hole. He smooths over the disturbed earth with the back edge of the loader, offers Willard a seat in the bucket, and sputters up the path to home.

Theron survives the lonely winter, but dies of a heart attack in the spring while cutting wood for a winter he'll never see.

ABOUT THE AUTHOR

Award-winning author and Vermont Public Radio commentator Bill Schubart first introduced us to these characters in his 2008 short story collection *The Lamoille Stories*.

FROM BILL: "The characters, eccentrics, and misadventures that make up these stories have always lived in me. Stories are a uniquely human aspect of our world. We are defined by the stories we tell, and as a writer I feel obliged not only to retell them to my children and grandchildren but to write them down."